Contemporary Chinese Poetry
in English Translation Series

Changyao
Selected Poems

Translated by Sun Jicheng and Ma Xiao

教育部人文社会科学重点研究基地
安徽师范大学中国诗学研究中心 组编
Chinese Poetry Research Center of Anhui Normal University

杨四平 主编　　上海文化出版社

当代汉诗英译丛书

昌耀诗歌英译选

孙继成　马晓 译

[英] 约翰·德鲁 审校

CONTENTS

目录

THE BORDER TOWN

In a border town. Night leaps down from the gate tower
To wander about in the wilderness.
— Baigafa, Baigafa, my love,
What flowers are you embroidering on your handkerchief?

(I'm embroidering mandarin ducks and butterflies, my love)

— Baigafa, Baigafa, my love,
Don't hide yourself away in your house. I have a
Beautiful cape for you!

Night leaps down from the battlements.
Leaps down, leaps down and wanders about in the wilderness.

July 25, 1957

边城

边城。夜从城楼跳将下来
踯躅原野。

——拜噶法，拜噶法，
你手帕上绣着什么花？

（小哥哥，我绣着鸳鸯蝴蝶花）

——拜噶法，拜噶法，
别忙躲进屋，我有一件
美极的披风！

夜从城垛跳将下来。
跳将下来跳将下来踯躅原野。

1957.7.25

THE HIGH CART

What is flapping its wings on this vast earth?...... It is the high cart. It is the Qinghai high cart. I respect them. But I cannot forget about them, more that they are heroes. And heroes cannot be forgotten.

Rising gradually from the horizon
It is the Qinghai high cart

Quietly rolling from the side of Big Dipper Palace
It is the Qinghai high cart

While rocking far away from the last time
It is still the Qinghai high cart

The Qinghai of the high cart, to me, is a mighty giant
The high cart of Qinghai, to me, is the giant's missing song

July 30, 1957 draft

高车

　　是什么在天地河汉之间鼓动如翼手？ ……是高车。是青海的高车。我看重它们。但我之难忘情于它们，更在于它们本是英雄。而英雄是不可被遗忘的。

从地平线渐次隆起者
是青海的高车

从北斗星宫之侧悄然轧过者
是青海的高车

而从岁月间摇撼着远去者
仍还是青海的高车呀

高车的青海于我是威武的巨人
青海的高车于我是巨人的轶诗

1957.7.30 初稿

ON THE SIDE OF MOUNT ERIDO SNOW PEAK

It is the top height I can conquer at this moment:

I pop out my head carefully

Amazed at the thin cliff there

The sun lingered for long towards the snow of Erido

Determine to jump into the sea and mountain with infinite gravity.

Stones sometimes slide down the slope with a great roar from top to bottom of the brown abyss,

Like battle cries of armies going far away. My knuckles are, like rivets,

Wedged into the gap between giant rocks. The blood oozes from the torn shoe sole under my feet.

Oh, how I wish an eagle or snow leopard could accompany me at this moment.

There is only a pitiful little spider on the eroded cliff

Enjoying quietly with me the gift from nature

Of happiness.

August 2, 1962

25

峨日朵雪峰之侧

这是我此刻仅能征服的高度了：
我小心翼翼探出前额，
惊异于薄壁那边
朝向峨日朵之雪彷徨许久的太阳
正决然跃入一片引力无穷的山海。
石砾不时滑坡引动棕色深渊自上而下一派喧鸣，
像军旅远去的喊杀声。我的指关节铆钉一般
楔入巨石罅隙。血滴，从脚下撕裂的鞋底渗出。
啊，此刻真渴望有一只雄鹰或雪豹与我为伍。
在锈蚀的岩壁但有一只小得可怜的蜘蛛
与我一同默享着这大自然赐予的
快慰。

1962.8.2

AT DUSK WHEN BARLEY BEER IS BREWED

At dusk when wheat wine is brewed,

The smoke from kitchen chimneys is drunk.

The alleys and laneways are drunk. The wind is

Also drunk.

On the riverbank, snowflakes are red.

The horse procession of the Zamashik tribe is marching out to welcome

the bride.

Towards their quivering silver fox fur hats,

The glacier in the distance gives the first great burst of laughter...

On a drunk morning,

The Zamashik people welcome back their God of Spring.

November 26, 1962

酿造麦酒的黄昏

酿造麦酒的黄昏，
炊烟陶醉了。巷陌陶醉了。风儿
也陶醉了。

河岸上，雪花是红的。
扎麻什克人迎亲的马队正在出征。
向着他们颤动的银狐皮帽，
冰河在远方发出了第一声大笑……

在醉了的早晨，
扎麻什克人迎回了自己的春神。

1962.11.26

ROW, ROW YOUR BOAT, FATHERS!
— TO BOATMEN IN THE NEW ERA

Ever since we understood the rhythm of waves,

Our antennae, they have, as definitely as this,

felt the lure of the sea:

— Row, row your boat,

Fathers!

We were born from the sea.

Our embryonic history

it is only our embryonic history

that has shown us the evolution from a fish egg to a civilized person.

We have cast off all our fins.

But we still row tenaciously.

But we still row strongly.

We are a group of men. We are a group of women.

We are a group of men

to whom the group of women is attached.

We pull on our oars and row just like this, just like this.

In the golden twilight of the sky's canopy,

So many overlapping shadows

seem drunk like proud soldiers at their victory feast.

We are not so far dead drunk.

划呀，划呀，父亲们！
—— 献给新时期的船夫

自从听懂波涛的律动以来，
我们的触角，就是如此确凿地
感受到大海的挑逗：

—— 划呀，划呀，
父亲们！

我们发祥于大海。
我们的胚胎史，
也只是我们的胚胎史 ——
展示了从鱼虫到真人的演化序列。
脱尽了鳍翅。
可是，我们仍在韧性地划呀。
可是，我们仍在拼力地划呀。
我们是一群男子。是一群女子。
是为一群女子依恋的
一群男子。
我们摇起棹橹，就这么划，就这么划。
在天幕的金色的晨昏，
众多仰合的背影
有庆功宴上骄军的醉态。
我们不至于酩酊。

The most passionate shouts,

are they our howls as we dash forward

along the curving horizon of the sea?

We are all born crying into this colourful universe.

The smiles we learn after birth are the consolation we repay our mothers.

— Crying and laughing,

We row from the sea to the inland river, to the continent...

We row from the continent to the sea, to the sky vault...

We paid a visit to the battlements of the Great Wall.

We learned for ourselves of the twelve galleons sunk in Quanzhou Bay.

We played a set of chimes from the late Spring and Autumn periods.

We read all the official books of history, even the oldest ones.

I heard the flowing waters of history in all containers.

I heard rebellious footsteps on the flowing waters.

— Row, fathers,

Row your boat!

There is time for us to hasten on our way.

The sun has not grown old yet; it's just at the noon of life.

We will have our own milestones.

We should have our own milestones.

But those whirlpools,

those ferocious ripples,

never give up stalking us,

with a single sweep

will take away our fathers and brothers forever,

twisting

the survivors' spines.

最动情的呐喊
莫不是我们沿着椭圆的海平面
一声向前冲刺的
嗥叫？

我们都是哭着降临到这个多彩的寰宇。
后天的笑，才是一瞥投报给母亲的慰安。
——我们是哭着笑着
从大海划向内河，划向洲陆……
从洲陆划向大海，划向穹窿……
拜谒了长城的雉堞。
见识了泉州湾里沉溺的十二桅古帆船。
狎弄过春秋末代的编钟。
我们将钦定的史册连根儿翻个。
从所有的器物我听见逝去的流水。
我听见流水之上抗逆的脚步。

——划呀，父亲们，
　　划呀！

还来得及赶路。
太阳还不见老，正当中年。
我们会有自己的里程碑。
我们应有自己的里程碑。
可那旋涡，
那狰狞的弧圈，
向来不放松对我们的跟踪，
只轻轻一扫
就永远地卷去了我们的父兄，
把幸存者的脊椎
扭曲。

Oh sea, I should curse your cruelty.

But the sea is not the sea without

its brutal ruthlessness. When boatmen lose the sea,

They are no longer

boatmen.

And so, we still light our torches happily.

We still must make baby clothes with passion in our hearts.

We row in high spirits... Ha-ha... row

... Ha-ha... row...

We crossed from the ice age to flood season.

From the equatorial winds to volcanic ash.

We crossed debris flows. Crossed

the traces of primitive communes and

sedimentary layers of biological remains...

We originally rowed here from a wild epoch.

We brought about a Da Yu,

he was already the God controlling the flood. And the upright girl

turned into the Jingwei bird filling up the sea.

There have already been many prophets.

There will always be land for olive branches to grow.

There will always be kingdoms to rush out from certainty.

But the lifespan of each of us is fleeting,

Hardly to witness Halley's Comet twice.

In another future from an immemorial time,

We will no longer recognize our transformed descendants.

大海，我应诅咒你的暴虐。
但去掉了暴虐的大海不是
大海。失去了大海的船夫
也不是
船夫。

于是，我们仍然开心地燃起爝火。
我们依然要怀着情欲剪裁婴儿衣。
我们昂奋地划呀……哈哈……划呀
……哈哈……划呀……
是从冰川期划过了洪水期。
是从赤道风划过了火山灰。
划过了泥石流。划过了
原始公社的残骸，和
生物遗体的沉积层……
我们原是从荒蛮的纪元划来。
我们造就了一个大禹，
他已是水边的神。
而那个烈女
变作了填海的精卫鸟。
预言家已经不少。
总会有橄榄枝的土地。
总会冲出必然的王国。
但我们生命的个体都尚是阳寿短促，
难得两次见到哈雷彗星。
当又一个旷古后的未来，
我们不再认识自己变形了的子孙。

But we still row tenaciously.

But we still row strongly.

On this shrinking planet,

There won't be another smoother road to go on.

There won't be any other choice.

Apart from five giant boats,

I only see boatmen yearning for the seashore.

    There are only shouts for the shore

    along the elliptical sea level

    combining into one

    untiring

    Howl.

Oh sea, you will never be moved to feel.

And our oars will never be dumb.

Our mothers and wives will pickle vegetables for winter still.

Our girls will still want to have a smart hairstyle.

Our fetuses will still be born of blood

and light.

可是，我们仍在韧性地划呀。
可是，我们仍在拼力地划呀。
在这日趋缩小的星球，
不会有另一条坦途。
不会有另一种选择。
除了五条巨大的舳舻，
我只看到渴求那一海岸的船夫。

　　只有啼呼海岸的呐喊
　　沿着椭圆的海平面
　　组合成一支
　　不懈的
　　噪叫。

大海，你决不会感动。
而我们的桨叶也决不会喑哑。
我们的婆母还是要腌制过冬的咸菜。
我们的姑娘还是要烫一个流行的发式。
我们的胎儿还是要从血光里
临盆。

... Is now a good time?

Are so many infants born into this world?

I really can't bear to hear infants crying.

But our oars are wholly reliable.

We just row like this. Row like this,

This is how we respond to the seduction of the sea:

— Row, Row, fathers!

Fathers!

Fathers!

We are not so far dead drunk.

We will go on our way with infants crying.

At the end of the sea

There will be our

Laughter...

October 6-29, 1981

……今夕何夕？
会有那么多临盆的孩子？
我最不忍闻孩子的啼哭了。
但我们的桨叶绝对地忠实。
就这么划着。就这么划着。
就这么回答着大海的挑逗：

——划呀，父亲们！
父亲们！
父亲们！

我们不至于酩酊。
我们负荷着孩子的哭声赶路。
在大海的尽头
会有我们的
笑。

1981.10.6—29

The Stag's Antlers

On the skull of a stag, there are two

small branches nourished by blood and essence.

In the faint light of fog

these high and crooked branches are bright and precious,

escaping over dangerous cliffs and marshes

to fight with hunters for survival.

Several centuries later, they are displayed on my bookshelf.

Among the new collection, I hear

A shot of a gun from the depth of the highland.

What a tragedy!

That setting sun shines on the call of the wilderness.

From high on the rocks, flying antlers suddenly fell to the ground...

Solemn and stirring.

March 2, 1982

鹿的角枝

在雄鹿的颅骨，生有两株
被精血所滋养的小树。雾光里
这些挺拔的枝状体明丽而珍重，
遁越于危崖沼泽，与猎人相周旋。

若干个世纪以后，在我的书架，
在我新得的收藏品之上，才听到
来自高原腹地的那一声火枪。——
那样的夕阳倾照着那样呼唤的荒野。
从高岩，飞动的鹿角，猝然倒仆⋯⋯
⋯⋯是悲壮的。

1982.3.2

Reflections: On the Western Highland

On the western mountains, that man
hears a bell ring like a buzz of years
in the frost. So lonely.

Who is speaking in the air:
— Ah, how slowly the secular time goes!
It seems to me that
it is yesterday that the Gaoche tribe came from the northern desert to the
western frontier land,
The reputation of General Ban Chao in the Han dynasty and his 36
military followers
could be still heard all the way,
But the late-comers
could you still have the chance to hear a beauty play the Chinese lute
behind her neck presented in Dunhuang County?

So lonely.
At 7:00 am, in the wild,
Only a jeep is running forward.
— In the distance
the yellow sand hill
is as bright as dusk.

July 1982

所思：在西部高原

西部的山。那人儿
听见霜寒里留有岁月嗡嗡不绝的
钟鸣。太寂寞。

是谁在空中作语：
——啊，世俗的光阴走得好慢！
我似乎觉得
高车部自漠北拓荒西来尚是昨天的事，
汉将军班超与三十六吏士的口碑
也还依然一路风闻，
可你们后来者
还听得敦煌郡献歌伎女反手弹琵琶么？

太寂寞。
凌晨七时的野岭
独有一辆吉普往前驱驰。
——远方
黄沙丘
亮似黄昏。

1982.7

SNOW. THE SONG OF A TIBETAN WOMAN, HER MAN AND THREE CHILDREN

1. Spring Tide: Her Dreamlike Hymn

In the snow in cold Xiqiang on New Year's Eve,

A Tibetan woman stands by the window decked with snowflakes,

With Her thin husband, three children

singing an ancient song in chorus:

— Gudergu, pump the bellows,

Lamb's ribs are cooked in the pot…

The sound is of an unforgettable, dreamlike

Hymn —

Gudergu, pump the bellows,

Lamb's ribs are cooked in the pot…

A toothless child stands on the top of the roof …

On this night, from the hellish basement, a turbulent

Spring tide rushes out, and the ancient Tibetan ballad lights the house

with its frosted window. I see icebergs melt in this temporal world,

and the colorful branches of fir trees fade and drip.

That night when the sun just goes down,

The chicks under the snowdrift have begun

to wake up in the morning.

雪。土伯特女人和她的男人及三个孩子之歌

1. 春潮：她的梦一般的赞美诗

西羌雪域。除夕。
一个土伯特女人立在雪花雕琢的窗口，
和她的瘦丈夫、她的三个孩子
同声合唱着一首古歌：
—— 咕得尔咕，拉风匣，
锅里煮了个羊肋巴……

是那么忘情的、梦一般的
赞美诗呵 ——
咕得尔咕，拉风匣，
锅里煮了个羊肋巴，
房上站着个尕没牙……

那一夕，九九八十一层地下室汹涌的
春潮和土伯特的古谣曲洗亮了这间
封冻的玻璃窗。我看到冰山从这红尘崩溃，
幻变五色的杉树枝由漫漶消融而至滴沥。
那一夕太阳刚刚落山，
雪堆下面的童子鸡就开始
司晨了。

2. My Palmprint Like Soaked Moss

She comes from her mother's home and brings back their ancestral
antiques for me:
a copper horse pendant and a coin in the Qing Dynasty from the dowry
of her old mother,
inscribes with characters "Qianlong Tongbao" that she picks out secretly.

She brings the news the shanty where we herd far beyond the snow line
had collapsed, but the pigsty built on the cliff is still intact.
She says that the mud wall was still full of my palm prints
like rows of suffering shells
in the soaked moss.

She says that these old shells make her
so sad.

2. 我的掌模浸透了苔丝

她从娘家来，替我捎回了祖传的古玩：
一只铜马坠儿，和一只从老阿娅的妆奁
偷偷摘取的"乾隆通宝"。

说我们远在雪线那边放牧的棚户已经
坍塌，唯有筑在崖畔的猪舍还完好如初。
说泥墙上仍旧嵌满了我的手掌模印儿，
像一排排受难的贝壳，
浸透了苔丝。

说我的那些古贝壳使她如此
难过。

3. In the Snowfield. At the Intersection of one Halo and Another

A Yak: A breeding ox.

He has long black, brown belly hair and white eyebrows.

He has a golden nose ring and golden horns.

The shallow hair on his forehead covers a pair of big eyes.

When he runs straight down from the snowy slope,

His tail is always higher and straight than other oxen's,

Like a proud Chinese fan palm,

floating among that black wave of tails,

floating at the forefront of that black wave.

Black waves

have contaminated the white snow.

This is a breeding ox, a yak.

At this moment, he enjoys walking north of the mountain.

On his upraised withers,

he carries a leather bag of barley, his reward from the shepherd.

He doesn't like this symbol.

Looking back, he sees the colorful, beautiful cow in the stable

still staring at him,

with her gentle eyes.

3. 在雪原。在光轮与光轮的交错之上

牦牛：一头种公牛。
它有褐黑的腹长毛和洁白的眉毛。
它有金黄的鼻圈和金黄的犄角。
额上的披发浅浅覆盖住了两只大眼睛。
当它从积雪的坡头率先直奔而下，
牛伙里它的后尾总是翘得比谁的都高挺，
像一株傲岸的蒲葵，
浮立在那一片黑色的波动。
浮立在那一片黑色波动的最前沿。
黑色的波动呀
污染着白雪……

这是一头种公牛，一头牦牛。
此刻它漫步在山阴。耸起的鬐甲
驮负着牧人酬谢它的一皮袋稞麦。
它不喜欢这一象征。
回过头去，看到厩栏中那只俏丽的
花母牛还在朝它凝望，
那眼神是温柔的。

Then, it seems I think

I hear the ox calling the cow again.

He seems as if I see the beautiful cow approaching.

I see a halo of light rising from the head of the cow.

I see hundreds and thousands of halos rising from all the cows'

heads.

From white snow to black waves,

at the intersection of the halos

appears the unique pair of horns

of the breeding ox.

于是，我恍若又
听到了公牛呼唤母牛的叫声。
恍若看到那只俏丽的花牛向这边靠拢。
看到一圈光轮从这只母牛的头顶升起。
看到成百、成千圈光轮从母牛群全体
成员的头顶升起。
从白雪、从黑色的波动，
在光轮与光轮的交错之上
是种公牛所独具的一轮
雄性的
犄角。

4. The History of Two Girls

A little fat girl. With bare buttocks

A fat girl rests nearby the fence.

The little girl creeps forward with high spirits.

She stops again and rests nearby the fence. Her bare buttocks

Leave a trail of scratches on the tender grass.

The little girl smiles excitedly and seriously

Calls every man passing by "Daddy."

In return for a silent smile, they walk away.

There is a domesticated pheasant on the grassland

pecking food with other poultry.

Behind the fence

the girl's Tibetan mother also smiles quietly.

Remembering that she used to be another girl on the grassland,

a little girl wears a pair of turquoise earrings,

a little girl possesses three Indian suitcases,

a little Tibet girl wears a green gown,

bouncing and dancing on spring grass. Seventeen young hunters gathered around her

throw their tributes of frogs to her by turn.

These thrown frogs are flying in the sky.

She picks up two corners of her gown and jumps lightly.

Those frogs, those victims,

the big grave of frogs sheds these hunters' tears in

Laughing.

Time,

you dominate everything!

4. 两个女孩的历史

小小的胖女孩儿。光腚的
一个胖女孩儿，歇在篱墙边。
这小女孩儿兴冲冲地朝前爬行。
又停住了。歇在篱墙边。屁股蛋儿
在嫩草地上蹭出一溜拖曳的擦痕。
小女孩儿兴冲冲地笑着，认真地
把每个过路的男子唤作"爸爸"。
报以无声的笑，他们走了过去。
草滩里有一只驯化的山雉
随着家禽啄食。

篱墙背后
女孩儿的土伯特母亲也悄悄地笑着。
忆起自己原是草滩里的另一个女孩儿，
一个佩戴松石耳环的小女孩儿，
一个富有三只印度皮箱的小女孩儿，
一个身著绿布长袍的土伯特小女孩儿，
正弹跳于春草。十七个少年猎手围拢来
将贡礼轮番向她的怀中投去。
投去的那些蛤士蟆在天空飞着。
她提起两只袍角轻盈地跳着。
那些蛤士蟆，那些牺牲品，
那些蛤士蟆的大坟冢有他们带笑的
泪水。

时间呵，
你主宰一切！

5. Sunshine: The Color of Fire: Warmth

From under the snow-covered hay-ricks

emits the fragrance of sunlight.

Here sunshine's the smell

of wheat straw.

In a spruce forest

The white feathers and bright red cockscombs of snowcocks pass with a

flash.

I think of the snow and the wildfire in the snowfield.

I think of the burning clouds falling on the west horizon.

And I think of the warmth of the fire.

Here: the color of fire is warmth.

The grass ash on the cattle stall is also warm.

So is the old cow's lowing.

And so is the decomposed dung grass.

On warm days,

the hunter bends over and runs across the shining field.

His steel lunch box hanging on his belt clatters.

The small copper spoon in the refined steel lunch box clatters.

5. 阳光：火的颜色：温暖

残雪覆盖的麦垛下面
散发出阳光的香气。
这里：阳光就是香气。
就是麦草秆儿。

落叶林里
闪过雪鸡的白翎羽和鲜红的鸡冠子。
我想起了白雪和雪地上的野火。
想起了西天沉落的火烧云。
想起了火的温暖。
这里：火的颜色就是温暖。

但是，垫在牛栏的草木灰同样温暖。
老牛哞哞的叫声同样温暖。
腐熟了的粪草同样温暖。

在温暖的日子，
猎人弯腰奔过亮晶晶的田野。
他的吊在腰带上的钢精饭盒哗啦啦响。
搁在钢精饭盒的小铜匙子哗啦啦响。

A shining hunter who stoops over the field
smells the sunshine under the hay ricks,
sees the red crests of snow cocks in the spruce forest,
hears the old cattle lowing on the river bank.

The hunter bends over and runs across the field. Shining.
His double-barreled shotgun has never been loaded with grapeshot.
He doesn't need to shoot.

I don't need to shoot. Some painters with sketches go with me and
come back from the wild. The people who welcome us
are my Tibetan wife and three children.

November 12-18, 1982 draft

从田野弯腰奔过的亮晶晶的猎人
嗅到了麦垛下面阳光的香气。
看到了落叶林里雪鸡的红冠子。
听到了河岸上老牛哞哞的叫声。

猎人弯腰奔过田野。亮晶晶的。
他的双筒猎枪从未装压过霰弹。
他并不需要射击。

我并不需要射击。有写生画家与我一同
从野外归来。欢迎我们的
是我的土伯特妻子和三个孩子。

1982.11.2—18 初稿

BORDER PASS: 24 LAMPS

A grand and large stadium, a brand-new children's park, and an unprecedented iron tower—24 lamps- formed the pride of the ancient city of Xining in the early 1980s. Citizens, tourists, and nomadic guests from the grasslands all enjoy their "trip to the West Gate."

The high-rise building—also called 24 lamps—stands in the center of this prosperous district, which inspired me. How beautiful it is made of: Metals and glasses. Rising like a canopy and floating in midair.

I once asked a poet from afar if he had noticed the grand building under construction at that time. He asked: "Isn't that the umbrella tower?" I smiled: "No, that's the tower of lights. It's our pride—the building of 24 lamps! "

1

Border Pass.
An unprecedented steel tree stands in the sky with many star-like lamps.
— Those birds under the canopy are 24 lamps!

Sun sets. The darkening earth becomes bright again in a sudden because of these birds.

边关：24 部灯

一座规模恢宏的体育馆、一座全新的儿童公园、一座前所未有的铁塔——24 部灯，构成了 80 年代初古城西宁的骄傲。市民、旅行者、从草原来的游牧族宾客都以"去西门口"一游为乐。

正是矗立在这繁华区中心的高层建筑——24 部灯——唤起了我的灵感。多么美：金属与玻璃。菌盖般膨起，浮在半空。

我曾经问一位远方来访的诗人可曾注意到当时尚在施工中的这座建筑。他说："那不是伞塔吗？"我笑了："不，那是灯的塔。是我们的——24 部灯！"

1

边关。
旷古未闻的一幢钢铁树直矗天宇宏观的星海。
——树冠下的那些栖鸟是 24 部灯吗！

日落。渐次转暗的大地因这些鸟儿生发之皓光忽地又亮了。

2

We gathered in the square.

Our teenagers are strolling on the beautiful lawn.

We can not be recognized whose descendants we are !?

Our ancestors might be soldiers at the borders. Or inhabitants of a border area. Or convicts.

Or female singers. Or travelling merchants. Or princes or their children.

But we are ourselves, after all.

We are all so handsome.

Ah, these foreheads.

Teeth laughing excitedly.

These salutes with eyes... All these are for our new construction of 24 lamps?

3

The eulogists said: Highly

In the plane of the hemisphere

24 lamps have been arranged as lotus seeds

which is the symbol of 24 hours that bring us vitality.

They are 24 golden flowers.

They are 24 golden cups.

2

我们云集广场。
我们的少年在华美如茵的草坪上款款踱步。
看不出我们是谁的后裔了？
我们的先人或是戍卒。或是边民。或是刑徒。
或是歌女。或是行商贾客。或是公子王孙。
但我们毕竟是我们自己。
我们都是如此英俊。

啊，这些额头。
激动地笑着的牙齿。
这些注目礼。……通通是为了我们新建的
24 部灯么？

3

追求者说：高高地
在那个半球体平面
按照莲子排列的 24 部灯
是给我们带来了生机的 24 个时辰之象征。

是 24 朵金花。
是 24 只金杯。

4

I am also a pursuer.

In the beginning, I have studied this scene very solemnly:

I have witnessed the construction team, like artists working from beginning to end

I have witnessed them set up three steel tripods

in the foundation pit. I have witnessed a workman climb on it

and connect another steel pipe to the connecting tenon. I have witnessed a workwoman

Climb up along the steel pipe

And connect a steel pipe to another tenon.

They firmly led the tentacles of the earth to the high altitude one tenon by another.

The high place is clear and clean. It is incandescent cloudy. It is a fluttering sky.

— Can you see any sails in the Pacific?

It was the first time that I heard about 24 lamps in this exciting building.

5

A shepherd girl came to the city for sightseeing.

Quietly she took off her earrings and hid them,

Then took them out and wore this pair again,

Finally, did she realize that such silver ornaments also match 24 lamps?

Did they look harmonious and well-matched on such a night?

Shiny earrings.

And shiny 24 bright lamps.

4

我也是追求者。
当初，我原极为庄重地研究了这一幕：
自始至终目睹施工队的艺术家们
从他们浇筑的基坑竖起三根鼎足而立的
钢管。看见一个男子攀援而上
将一根钢管衔接在榫头。看见一个女子
沿着钢管攀援而上，将一根钢管
衔接在另一根榫头。
他们坚定地将大地的触角一节一节引向高空。
高处是晴岚。是白炽的云朵。是飘摇的天。
—— 看得到太平洋的帆吗？
那时，我才第一次打听到这振奋人心的
24 部灯。

5

进城来观光的牧羊女，
你将耳坠悄悄摘下了藏起，
又将藏起的耳坠悄悄取出戴上，
最终是意识到了这样的银饰与这样的 24 部灯，
相映在这样的夜里也是和谐的、是般配的么？

亮闪闪的耳坠。
亮闪闪的 24 部灯。

6

But how can I relate these 24 lamps to 24 sound parts on
the belly of an insect? How can I think of a singing cicada?

I thought of the singing champion —
24 lamps.

7

And I finally feel like I am a tiny water drop.
I feel dizzy. I feel like the waves ripple. I feel I am flowing.

Ah, flowing rivers!
These are rivers: Two broad, confident and self-respecting
Rivers of men converge here and rush forward.
I noticed a ship with a painted logo of "Alpinists' Cub of H Province."
Sailing to the snow mountain of Animaqing.
The ice drops of that holy mountain flow to the boats in the Yellow River.
They float to the Pacific Ocean.

I am sure it is 24 lamps that light up our tall tree
from behind.

August to October, 1983

6

但我怎么会从 24 部灯想到昆虫腹下的
24 块发声板呢？怎么会想到唱歌的蝉？

我想到了歌王 ——
24 部灯。

7

而我感到自己是一滴水了。
感到晕眩。感到在荡漾。在流动。

啊，河流！
这是河流：两条雄阔而充满自信、自尊的
人的河流在此交汇，又奔向遥远。
我注意到有一部涂有"H 省登山协会"标志的
船，将驶向阿尼玛卿雪山。
那座圣山的冰滴是通向黄河之舟的。
是通向太平洋的。

确信从后面照亮我们的高树
必是 24 部灯……

1983.8—10

THE RIVERBED
(ONE OF THE SHAPES OF THE QINGHAI TIBET PLATEAU)

I walked down from the white-headed Bayankala Mountains.

A white-headed snow leopard lay silently in the eagle's castle, watching me go far away.

But I am prouder of myself.

I heard the Tanguts' carriages move at a long distance.

I smiled quietly without making a single sound.

I let those wagons on the road early go along my embankment one after another.

The wagons' wheels again the stones on the ground sounded like horns to welcome God, climbing up on my chest,

The wheels beat against my bulging muscles.

The Tangut wagoners in their heavy winter clothes also accompanied their horses

Raised their steps cautiously and were ready to pull the braking halters firmly in their hands at any time.

They said I was a riverbed like a giant lying down.

They said I was a riverbed, like a giant standing up.

河床
（《青藏高原的形体》之一）

我从白头的巴颜喀拉走下。
白头的雪豹默默卧在鹰的城堡，目送我走向远方。
但我更是值得骄傲的一个。
我老远就听到了唐古特人的那些马车。
我轻轻地笑着，并不出声。
我让那些早早上路的马车，沿着我的堤坡，鱼贯而行。
那些马车响着刮木，像奏着迎神的喇叭，登上了我的胸脯。
轮子跳动在我鼓囊囊的肌块。
那些裹着冬装的唐古特车夫也伴着他们的辕马
谨小慎微地举步，随时准备拽紧握在他们手心的刹绳。

他们说我是巨人般躺倒的河床。
他们说我是巨人般屹立的河床。

Yes, I walked down from the white-headed Bayankara Mountains. I am a moist riverbed,

I am a dried riverbed and a vast and mighty riverbed.

My name resounds in people's ears.

I am solid, broad and magnificent. I am a fully developed male beauty.

I am creative and constantly

I discharge my inexhaustible energy into the eastern sea.

I tattoo my skin so the carefully displayed figures can be appreciated far away rather than close to approaching.

I like to tell frost and wind how hairy my body is.

I let ten thousand mountains open their caves so the beloved waters can be put into my bosom of love.

I'm a father.

I love to hear the condor give a long cry. He has the voice of a teenager, and his eyes have the charm of a girl's eyes.

The dance of his wings like wheels can make the blood boil.

I praise the hunter who lurks in the deep snow of my past for the whole night.

And equally appreciate the three-legged mother wolf.

She limps from my shadow to the clouds in the sky every evening in the long summer.

I will always miss you all, the vanished Yellow River Elephant.

是的，我从白头的巴颜喀拉走下。我是滋润的河床，
我是枯干的河床，我是浩荡的河床。
我的令名如雷贯耳。
我坚实宽厚、壮阔，我是发育完备的雄性美。
我创造，我须臾不停地
向东方大海排泻我那不竭的精力。
我刺肤纹身，让精心显示的那些图形可被仰观而不可近狎。
我喜欢向霜风透露我体魄之多毛。
我让万山洞开，好叫钟情的众水投入我博爱的襟怀。

我是父亲。
我爱听秃鹰长喉，他有少年的声带，他的目光有少女的媚眼。
他的翼轮双展之舞可让血流沸腾。
我称誉在我隘口的深雪潜伏达旦的那个猎人。
也同等地欣赏那头三条腿的母狼。
她在长夏的每一次黄昏都要从我的阴影跂向天边的彤云。
也永远怀念你们 —— 消逝了的黄河象。

I'll see you at the same time at every moment.

In every moment, I show myself as a thousand people.

I am a crooked mountain peak, a sunken fault and an incised isthmus.

I am a dizzy hurricane.

I am a longitudinal riverbed. I am a horizontal riverbed. I am the main melody of the score.

I have brocade, jewelry and gold all over my body.

I stretch like a bow; I open up virgin soil thousands of miles.

I am time, an ancient site, a piece of palatal bone fossil of the universe. I am the first emperor.

I am the sail wall in the array, the square, the large city, and the unfolding landscape. I am an unfathomable abyss.

I am a structural force and a gallop. I am a goal that can't be overcome.

I put the image of the dragon back on the front stage of the world.

But now I still turn to your white-headed Bayankara.

Your wagons have been loaded with Kunshan jade and heading back home.

Your wheat seed lights up on time in the peasant woman's callow palm.

Your full moon is rising from my navel.

I promised you that the tide flood will come soon,

And the tide flood has come.

March 22 to April 20, 1984

我在每一个瞬间都同时看到你们。
我在每一个瞬间都表现为大千众相。
我是屈曲的峰峦，是下陷的断层，是切开的地峡。
是眩晕的飓风。
是纵的河床。是横的河床。是总谱的主旋律。
我一身织锦，一身珠宝，一身黄金。
我张弛如弓，我拓荒千里。
我是时间，是古迹，是宇宙洪荒的一片腭骨化石。是始皇帝。
我是排列成阵的帆墙，是广场，是通都大邑，是展开的景观。是
不可测度的深渊。
是结构力，是驰道。是不可克的球门。
我把龙的形象重新推上世界的前台。

而现在我仍转向你们白头的巴颜喀拉。
你们的马车已满载昆山之玉，走向归程。
你们的麦种在农妇的胝掌准时地亮了。
你们的团圆月正从我的脐蒂升起。

我答应过你们，我说潮汛即刻到来，
而潮汛已经到来……

1984.3.22—4.20

GIANT SPIRIT

In a western city. On Xiguan (West Pass) Bridge. Year after year,

I witness the Nanchuan River become fleshy and plump in summer,

And turn thin and desolate in autumn.

In my favorite fortress, there is a pinch of snow that never melts,

which is the lofty ice peak of Qilian Mountain.

The Dayuezhi people were forced to march to the west once they set up

their wandering yurts there.

I have repeatedly reneged on my promise to postpone my visit to the icy

peak.

Over the years, did the gale in Alike snowfield

Still, remember my unbound hair when I was a child?

In fact, I never left that mountain range,

In the dreams of harvesting the treasures of copper, barley and musk stag

I have always sharpened a sickle in the newly reclaimed land.

巨灵

西部的城。西关桥上。一年年
我看着南川河夏日里体态丰盈肥硕，
而秋后复归清瘦萧索。
在我倾心的关塞有一撮不化的白雪，
那却是祁连山高洁的冰峰。
被迫西征的大月氏人曾在那里支起游荡的穹庐。
我已几次食言推迟我的访问。
日久，阿力克雪原的大风
可还记得我年幼的飘发？
其实我何曾离开过那条山脉，
在收获铜石、稞麦与雄麝之宝的梦里
我永远是新垦地的一个磨镰人。

The ancient battlefield retreated behind me at an accelerated speed,

Old friends mostly look at me and smile without saying anything.

May I ask? Who loves this land the most?

The ravines on the forehead of amorous people have been widening yearly.

Children laughed at the thorny white beard on my chin.

I will be the echo of ancient history.

I will be the iron that is buried in the soil. I will be this calcium. I will be the phosphorus

But the giant spirit always calls on people not to be frozen and numb:

The "golden section" of beauty is realized by constant changes,

Life comes from "symmetry breaking."

Be shiny! The vast expanse of land covered with red satin,

In your temple of the Yellow River God, the hand of the giant spirit

has created these worshipped gluttonous beasts, phoenix birds, Kui dragons...

Only the eggshells of the gods of the old country deserve such respect and worship.

The higher I climbed up, the closer I found Midway Island.

The horizon is far away, and the offshore has been completed in the continental shelf.

The brilliance of the universe always has a frequency resonating with me.

Can you feel such a great shock?

古战场从我身后加速退去，
故人多半望我笑而不语。
请问：这土地谁爱得最深？
多情者额头的万仞沟壑正逐年加宽。
孩子笑我下颏已生出几枝棘手的白刺。
我将是古史的回声。
是逸漏于土壤的铁质。是这钙。这磷……
但巨灵时时召唤人们不要凝固僵滞麻木：
美的"黄金分割"从常变中悟得，
生命自"对称性破缺"中走来。

照耀吧，红缎子覆盖的接天旷原，
在你黄河神的圣殿，是巨灵的手
创造了这些被膜拜的饕餮兽、凤鸟、夔龙……
唯化育了故国神明的卵壳配享如许的尊崇。

我攀登愈高，发觉中途岛离我愈近。
视平线远了，而近海已毕现于陆棚。
宇宙之辉煌恒有与我共振的频率。
能不感受到那一大摇撼？

You always feel restless.

We observed an ancient solar eclipse from the tortoiseshell of the ruins of
the Yin Dynasty.

We searched the ancient river from the ancient books of sages.

We constantly calibrate history in history.

We are constantly changing history in history.

We can appreciate all its solemn and stirring sense of the mission

Due to the call of a giant spirit.

I have no regrets.

Until the last minute comes.

September 9, 1984

总要坐卧不宁。
我们从殷墟的龟甲察看一次古老的日食。
我们从圣贤的典籍搜寻湮塞的古河。
我们不断在历史中校准历史。
我们在历史中不断变作历史。
我们得以领略其全部悲壮的使命感
是巨灵的召唤。

没有后悔。
直到最后一分钟。

1984.9.9 写毕

THAT PERSON

In such a silence — whose sigh do you hear?

The storm on the Mississippi River is now climbing and walking there.
On the other end of the earth, one sits alone without a word.

May 31, 1985

斯人

静极 —— 谁的叹嘘?

密西西比河此刻风雨,在那边攀缘而走。
地球这壁,一人无语独坐。

1985.5.31

ONE HUNDRED BULLS

1

The quick pace of one hundred bulls
turns into the echo of the rising friction in time.

Like curtains in the sky, the red clouds are as solemn and stirring as the
blood wine.

2

Horns raised,
They are isolated and independent.

Horns raised,
One hundred bulls and one hundred ninety-nine horns.
One hundred bulls raised one hundred and ninety-nine kinds of ferocity.
Stand up at Horn Fort with red clouds extending in the sky,
The bugler holds the broken horn in his hand
And whines it like weeping...

As solemn and stirring as the blood wine.

一百头雄牛

1

一百头雄牛噌噌的步伐。
一个时代上升的摩擦。

彤云垂天，火红的帷幕，血酒一样悲壮。

2

犄角扬起，
遗世而独立。

犄角扬起，
一百头雄牛，一百九十九只犄角。
一百头雄牛扬起一百九十九种威猛。
立起在垂天彤云飞行的牛角砦堡，
号手握持那一只折断的犄角
而呼呜呜……

血酒一样悲壮。

3

The testicles and scrotum of one hundred bulls cast their shadows onto the earth.

The testicles and scrotum of one hundred male cattle hang down in the sky.

At midnight, one hundred male hormones permeate into the soil,

As solemn and stirring as the bloody wine.

March 27, 1986

3

一百头雄牛低悬的睾丸阴囊投影大地。
一百头雄牛低悬的睾丸阴囊垂布天宇。
午夜，一百头雄性荷尔蒙穆穆地渗透了泥土。
血酒一样悲壮。

1986.3.27

LISTEN TO THE CALL: HURRY UP ON THE ROAD

1. The Sun

The sun says: I call you up.

Your first reply sounds lazy and easy.

And then, you hear the seductive word clearly. Hence, the emotional grease immediately lubricates your throat, and the solemn artificial whiskers then decorate your dissemble. You get up and act elegantly and romantically. When you pronounce, your voice sounds as plump as your strong chest, like a resonator. You sweep away all your tiredness and resume an inexhaustible stunning look.

After that, every answer you give has a profound meaning.

The sun says you will be a good athlete.

The sun says: You will be a good actor. A good stalking horse.

The sun says: Come on, go ahead.

听候召唤：赶路

1. 太阳

太阳说：我召唤你。
而你的第一声回答懒洋洋，漫不经心。
此后你听清了那个诱惑的词，于是情感的油脂立刻润滑你的嗓眼，
庄重的髯口随之矫饰你的假面。你起身，举态儒雅而风流。你每
一吐字归音都饱满如你共鸣箱似的雄实胸廓。你一扫全部怠倦而
有了用之不竭的飞扬神采。
此后你的每一声回答都富于深长意味。

太阳说，你会是一名好的竞技选手。
太阳说：你会是一名好演员。一匹好走马。

太阳说：来，朝前走。

2. The Canyon

Canyon, I hear the swift horseshoes

run close behind me. I don't want to be left behind.

And I hear the swift hooves like flying bats

running close behind me. I dare not slack off.

I hear the glacier break and flow for thousands of miles

while I may escape, crying out in alarm like tearing silk?

I feel that falling behind is inevitable for me.

Do I have the magic of invisibility all of a sudden?

Can I cast aside my shadow as easily as I strip away my clothes?

Can I turn into a cliff and unite with the pursuer?

I dare not slack off. I want to fly high. Yes, I fly high.

I jump over a gaping abyss,

the burial place of the five hundred fighters killed in their battle.

I fall down. But they finally approached me.

They step over my gaze and run away from me quickly.

Each rider is assigned two horses to ride.

They spread their arms and legs and fly with the horses, looking as lofty

as topless towers on city gates.

The iron hooves ignite flowering sparks at every instant.

I hear the hooves strike, flashing gold.

Finally, they take flight and disappear.

2. 峡谷

峡谷，我听到疾行的蹄铁
在我身后迫近。我不甘落伍。
而我听到疾行的蹄铁如飞掠的蝙蝠
在我身后迫近。我不敢懈怠。
我听到冰河破裂一泻千里，而我可能乘坐这裂帛似的一声惊呼逃
之夭夭？
我深感落伍已不可避免。
我可有隐身术？
我可如脱衣一般抛却身后的影子，
我可否化入迫逼的巉岩与追逼者合为一体！
我不敢懈怠。我欲飞翔。于是我就飞翔了。
我跃过一道深渊，察悟那窀穸就是临穴惴惴的五百甲士葬身之所。
我跌倒。而他们终于逼近。
他们跨越我的目光奔驰而去了。
每一骑士都兼领两匹备乘的马骑。
他们张开四肢与奔马一同腾飞，巍峨如叠次耸峙的城楼。
石火在每一瞬动的铁蹄绽开十字小花。
我听见马蹄磕碰如金箔弹跳脱落……终于去远了。

I feel my chest constricted by scratching thirst.

I collapse into the glacier, icicles stabbing my brain.

My fire-like tongue pokes into the glacier crevices and wind erosion for a
rush of predation, and then I spread out my limbs.

Then I hear the huge vibration of an engine.

I sit up, see a helicopter hover low at the canyon mouth at sunrise,

like a bamboo dragonfly,

like a tilted spinning gyro,

making the cold air around it radiate a circle of white light.

While I hear the swift hooves like flying bats approaching behind me.

我忽觉胸中陡然袭来一阵急待抓挠的焦渴。
我瘫倒在冰河，一种被陌生胸腔灼伤的颤栗锥刺脑髓。我以我的
火舌探入冰河风蚀的裂隙匆匆一阵掠食，而后摊平四肢。

而后我听见了引擎的巨大震动。
我坐起，见直升机穿行太阳初升的峡口低飞盘旋如一支竹蜻蜓，
如一只倾斜的陀螺，让周遭寒气放射一圈白光。
而我听到疾行的蹄铁如飞掠的蝙蝠又已在我身后迫近。

3. The Gold like Tiger Skin

Ah, macho attack!

Ah, sharp weapon! Ah, acute angle!

Ah, mountains and plains!

Ah, the road to gold!

Ah, burly chaps!

A gold digger flees in the shadow of the river,

hides gold dust secretly, takes a detour around, passes and goes across

the Gobi and comes down from snowy mountains.

He steps from the shade of the river.

Gold guides him forward.

Gold is his memory.

Gold is his tobacco.

Gold is his life and dream.

Gold is his wife and children.

Gold is his tenderness and gentleness.

Gold is his code for seniority and inferiority,

and his courage derives from his greed and lust for tiger skin.

The gold digger drives the golden tiger skin to retreat toward their

hometown in the shadow of the river.

3. 黄金虎皮

啊，雄性攻击！
啊，利器！啊，锐角！
啊，山野！
啊，黄金之路！
啊，彪形大汉！

在河的阴影通行的淘金者
秘藏金沙绕道关卡横穿戈壁从雪山下来了。
又从河阴踏去。
黄金为他引路。
黄金是记忆。是烟草。是生命与梦。是妻室儿女。是温柔敦厚。
是长幼尊卑，是色胆包天的黄金虎皮。
淘金者驱驰着黄金虎皮在河的阴影朝向故里通行。

Ah, the road to gold!

Ah, the old granny herding the sheep has removed a bright hot copper pot from her robe and is preparing her noon tea at the sunny cliff stone!

The gold diggers are late-comers who covet

the watershed leading to the golden land.

Crawling in the egg-shaped pebbled hut,

he can not cure his late lung disease and

catch hold of the golden tiger skin within reach.

Exhausted, he falls down from Heaven's threshold into the dust he was born from.

Ah, the sun has sunk on the road to gold!

Five gold diggers lose their gold dust, and

they embrace each other and cry on the cliff returning.

Three pieces of stone used by granny to make tea have turned cold.

The five gold diggers who lose the gold dust also feel cold.

They take each other's arms and say goodbye to the world and

jump from the cliff top, feeling that they are flying towards the moon.

The demon's kisses have already become the mushrooms that grow everywhere at the bottom of the gorge.

Ah, countless red hands shake, and golden tiger skins are driven away in the mountains.

Ah, the sea I have always yearned for shows the glory of that moment in the western sky.

啊，黄金之路！
啊，放牧羊群的老奶奶已从袍襟取出揣得亮热的铜罐在向阳崖石
升起午时的茶炊了！

后来的淘金者是觊觎的淘金者，
觊觎在通往金地的分水岭了。匍匐在卵石搭起的卵形小屋而不能
穿凿晚期肺气肿摘取伸手可及的黄金虎皮。而耗尽盘资从天堂的
门槛跌落生身的尘埃。
啊，太阳已经下沉在黄金之路！
啊，五个金沙失盗的淘金者已相抱痛哭在归来的山崖。老奶奶煨
茶的三片石冰凉了。金沙失盗的淘金者心地也冰凉了。五个淘金
者相挽从崖巅一声作别，感觉身子一齐向着月亮飞升。妖人的毒
吻已是峡底遍生的蘑菇。
啊，无数双红手摇撼，黄金虎皮在山里驱驰。

啊，我永在向往的海就在西天显现那一时的荣华了。

4. The Whiskers

You, the traveler

hold a chisel in your hand along the way

like a nameless sculptor seeks his ancestors in the West

and illuminate the gods you recast on the cliff, one after the another.

On the night of the barren wildness, you carefully feed your jacklight.

And does the jacklight not

refeed your whiskers late at night?

Your whiskers washed by fire look beautiful,

As soft and passionate as the thin moss near the pebbles

swaying slightly at the same rhythm as the ripples in the stream.

You don't notice your

whiskers you have taken good care of have not made you look tough and

intrepid as you expect, cunning as the west admire.

Your soft whiskers look as lovely and soft as a baby's downy hair.

Your eyes look tender as if freshly bathed and fresh as if soaped in a

bathtub.

And on your neck, a lace is

connected with two golden legs of a pair of sunglass on your chest,

Two blue lenses look very mysterious, like the two eyes of a sleeping

fish.

4. 络腮胡须

你，旅行者
沿途立起凿刀
以无名雕塑家西部寻根的爱火
——照亮摩崖被你重铸的神祇。
在荒城之夜你又精心喂养自己的篝灯了。
而篝灯
不是也在喂养你黉夜的一丛
络腮胡须?

你的
在火光洗濯下的胡须多美，如溪流圆石边缘随水纹微微摆动的薄
薄苔丝绵软而动情。
你不曾察觉
你苦心经营的胡须并未带来你所歆羡的犷悍或西部汉子狡黠的美
气质。
你柔柔的胡须可爱如婴孩耳际柔柔的胎毛。
你的眸子红嫩水鲜宛若刚自澡盆浴毕漂净皂沫。
而你项颈，一串吊链
将金丝腿变色镜垂挂胸襟，
蓝色镜片幽远如同鱼目之睡眠。

Ah, the whiskers of the western root seeker look at the moon

They are as old as an ox tendon.

The decayed city walls are smoothed by the western root seekers

like sheepskin book covers of the historical records.

The western root seekers listening to the wind,

hear a song sung by a long reed in the dunes.

The western root seeker

frozen by the time and tide

Looking back at the sentries of the historical paddocks

whose halos are crisscrossed,

As if he hears his long hair crying against the wind,

As if his single arm yells and stretches out of a bottleneck,

as if an iron tree is blooming.

A huge shoe-like ship is rushing towards the doomed reef of Jinsha River.

In the eyes of the sentimental

Among the statues of Stone Men in the Turkic Wilderness in Central Asia

Returning is the sail of Alien.

Ah ah ah, ah ah ah, ah ah ah. ah ah ah. ah ah ah,

ah ah ah, ah ah ah, ah ah ah, ah ah ah, ah ah…

White cranes fly north in the formation of whiskers toward the moon.

啊，西部寻根者望月的络腮胡须苍老已如牛筋。
西部寻根者抚平的城壁枯槁已如史籍之羊皮封。
听风的西部寻根者如闻沙丘中一部芦苇的长歌。
西部寻根者
自岁月的定格
反看历史围场的哨口
晕轮交错，
如闻自己的长发迎向朔风号泣，
如见呐喊的独臂探出瓶颈之外，
进如开花铁树。

巨大的一只屐履正冲向金沙江宿命的暗礁。
在感伤者眼底
中亚荒原突厥石人的造像
复归是外星人的风帆。

啊啊啊啊啊啊啊啊啊啊啊啊啊啊啊啊啊啊啊。
北去的白鹤在望月的络腮胡须如此编队远征。

5. The Bloody Route

It knocks at the door.

Its forelimbs rest on the threshold to support its chest.

Its backbone collapses like a broken snow cliff.

Its buttocks and tail are squeezed and stuck with its hind limbs,

a piece of useless meat dartos among bloodstains, dust and dirt.

Behind, it is night, a pain, an adventure not to be thought of.

It becomes quiet instead.

It trembles all of a sudden.

It lowers its head to lick its fur, stunningly beautiful like sparks.

It licks it for a long time,

like a frustrated person lovely combing a cloak he has to pawn,

It finally feels tired and squinted.

The whirlwind it has made is over.

However, at the moment, does its unconventional regained from suffering

match its nobility gained from its vigorous fight?

Its eyes open heavily,

It glances at the deep valley, the grand pass,

the plank road that haunted it in the cave...

Turning its head one way, it steps to the other, left, right, left, right...

In this way, it moves the only two forelegs alternately,

dragging the broken lower body like a piece of soft satin towards the
universal kindness of silence tolerance and fatefully heading for its
doomed food-hunting.

5. 血路

它来敲门。

它的前肢搁在门槛支撑两肋。

它的脊梁坍塌如雪崖崩陷。

它的臀尾与后肢挤压粘连成为一片无用肉膜夹带血污、草屑与尘埃附丽身后。

背后是夜，是不可细察的痛苦或冒险。

它反而宁静了。

它哆嗦了一下。

它低头舔舐自己胸脊那块曾经美丽得乱爆电火花的毛皮，—— 它的毛皮。它久久地舔舐，仿佛一个迫不得已而典当售卖自己大氅的失意者为心爱之物作最后梳理，

它终觉疲倦而眯闭起眼睛。

它的旋风结束了。

然而此刻它于磨难显示的超脱不也足以与它在雄健搏杀中曾经享有的高贵相匹配？

它睁开眼，沉重地

看了一眼屋宇内所曾出没的深谷、雄关或栈道……转过头去，向左迈出一步，就这样侧转身来交替移动仅存的两只前足拖曳起软缎般覆地的残破下体慢慢踱向灭寂包容的普遍仁慈，走向必定的觅食。

On the bloody route: There is an immigrant tribe that has traveled long distances.

On the bloody route: A mother who dies a bloody death on a saddled horse.

On the bloody route: A naked corpse is abandoned on the slope.

On the bloody route: A goat intestine far away from its limbs, plundered by a coyote.

The mother cuts off her memory of the moon's loneliness,
painful as she listens to Xiao, a vertical bamboo flute.

The grand earth
whose very name makes flowers open and roots grow every moment
Like green branches
Hanging in a dense forest
Before one day
They all at once fall into old age

The lamb's
sweet cry
becomes
a suffering trap
of its maternal love

The confused noise of the world of creatures
are full of the mystery of uncertainty.

血路：一支长途迁徙跋涉的部族。
血路：一个在鞍马血崩咽气的母亲。
血路：一具弃置坡头的裸尸。
血路：一条从肢下被山狗叼衔蜿蜒牵伸去远的羊肠。

母亲剪断月魄的记忆微痛如听箫。

大地
每刻落地开花生根的名字
像密林
悬挂的青枝
然后在某一天
同时衰老

羊羔
甜蜜的叫声
是母爱
苦难的
陷阱

物种世界的喧哗
测不准的玄机。

6. Love

Your trembling soft body
curled up in my crescent embrace
You are the seed of my universe
I am your pod

A feverish night
A stretched kiss
like a blind silkworm
expects to be fed
A beautiful moan
A pastoral song that makes the horizon bend suddenly
feasts your eyes with the dark green which appears once a thousand years

Pain is doomed
caused by the attack of love
Broken sparks fall into an endless loss
like a dead pigeon
like a river, a wound, a tree
As remote as reborn

6. 爱

你颤栗的软体
蜷缩在我新月形的合抱
你是我宇宙的涵蕴
我是你外具的介壳

热病似的黑夜
伸展的吻
似蚕宝盲目
期待赐食
美的呻吟
地平线蓦然弯曲的牧歌
供你赏尽千年一瞬的碧绿

注定痛苦
爱的撞击
破碎的火星堕入无穷的坠失
如殒命的飞鸽
如一条河、一次流血、一棵树
遥远如同再生

7. The Moon in the Water

The sun says: Come on, go ahead.
——From the First Chapter, "The Sun"

When the sun is setting,

Footprints

stagger.

Stagger… stagger.

When the sun is setting, the sea I always yearn for shows for a moment

in the western sky: Glory. Glory. Glory.

I watch the dark shadow of the rising red current in the distance change

and flow according to time series, drifting away like the island we never

know,

Like from village chimneys, the disorderly smoke.

Like dyed indigo pieces drying on the beach.

Like iron scraps bursting asunder under the forging hammer,

cooling and discoloring. …

A rushing traveler

moves on the vast sandbar

sighing, the remote time and space in his eyes

Are the unreachable moon in the water.

7. 水月

太阳说：来，朝前走。
—— 摘自首章《太阳》

太阳沉落时，
步印
飘荡。
飘荡。……飘荡。
太阳沉落时我永在向往的海就已在西天短暂地显现那一时的荣华。荣华。荣华。
我遥望红色海流不断升起来的暗影依时序幻化流变渐远如我们无闻的岛屿，如村烟纷扬零落。如靛蓝染布一匹匹摊晒海涂。如锻锤下一串串铁屑飞进冷却变色。……赶路的人
移步在浩瀚沙洲
喟叹眼中遥隔的时空
永是不可沟通的水月。

The rushing traveler is always rust reappearing between heaven and earth, lamenting he is too sluggish to extricate himself.

When the sun is setting, there are always rushing travelers on their way expecting a single bed for them to rest in.

Instantly
The ascus of the night has bridged everything.
But you are angered by loneliness,
run across your fear, and finally, climb over the straits of the bright moon,
feeling the long and short beats of the brass instruments in the sea
weaving a crown for twilight.

When the sun is setting, I worry about where to return for a rest.
When the sun is rising, the moon in the water hides not to be seen
I regain my courage for another expedition.

October 16, 1987

赶路的人永是天地间再现的一滴锈迹
慨叹无可自拔的臃滞。

太阳沉落时永有赶路的人
痴望一席归享自己的卧榻。

瞬时
夜的子囊
将一切弥合，而你已被孤独激怒穿越恐惧，终于攀登在明月的海
峡，感觉海洋铜管乐搏杀的节拍长短参差闪击
织为黎明之皇冠。

太阳沉落时我为归宿张皇。
太阳涌动时水月隐形
我重又再生出征之勇气。

1987.10.16 写毕

GRAND INLAND

An Inland. A vertical silhouette. At the headwaters of the river.
Who shares the golden twilight with me and retreats into the moon gem?

The lonely inland is grand, silent, empty, and eternal,
which makes all possible sensations deliquesced and perished from the
beginning
And it will become insignificant forever.
The lonely inland
is a silent fire,
and a silent collapse.

A disheveled traveler goes westward on the open highway. A blackened
aluminum rice pot is buttoned upside down on his backpack. A club is
used as a walking stick, held horizontally at his waist. His hair on the
temples is tied up. His grey hair looks like rabbit hair is mildewed. His
neck is bent forward like an ox carries his yoke. His opened pupils wide,
panting because of suffocation. My intuition is that his hunger is also my
hunger. My intuition is that his flesh is my flesh. The reason why he is
depressed is also mine, and my joy is not necessarily his.
But what is heavier is the loneliness of the soul.
Who shares the golden twilight with me and retreats into the moon gem?
A disheveled traveler carries his luggage across the grand highland.
There is no village. No Ridgefield. And no water wells.
The remote mountain is as rough as a waterproof cloth tightened up the
skeleton of a giant animal.
The swamp is scattered like a piece of bright green frog skin.
A challenged traveler walks on god's sand table.

内陆高迥

内陆。一则垂立的身影。在河源。
谁与我同享暮色的金黄然后一起退入月亮宝石?

孤独的内陆高迥沉寂空旷恒大
使一切可能的轰动自肇始就将潮解而失去弹性。
而永远渺小。
孤独的内陆。
无声的火曜。
无声的崩毁。

一个蓬头垢面的旅行者西行在旷远的公路,一只燎黑了的铝制饭
锅倒扣在他的背囊,一根充作手杖的棍棒横抱在腰际。他的鬓角
扎起。兔毛似的灰白有如霉变。他的颈弯前翘如牛负轭。他睁大
的瞳仁也似因窒息而在喘息。我直觉他的饥渴也是我的饥渴。我
直觉组成他的肉体的一部分也曾是组成我的肉体的一部分。使他
苦闷的原因也是使我同样苦闷的原因,而我感受到的欢乐却未必
是他的欢乐。
而愈益沉重的却只是灵魂的寂寞。
谁与我同享暮色的金黄然后一起退入月亮宝石?
一个蓬头的旅行者背负行囊穿行在高迥内陆。
不见村庄。不见田垄。不见井垣。
远山粗陋如同防水布绷紧在巨型动物骨架。
沼泽散布如同鲜绿的蛙皮。
一个挑战的旅行者步行在上帝的沙盘。

At the headwater of the river

A group of standing travelers look up at the sky, hold wine bottles in their

hands, and drink like a fish,

and throw the empty bottles towards the high road under their feet.

It is a mock religious sacrifice.

The fragments on the ground looked like scales and shells and moved

into tears.

The grand inland is floating.

December 12, 1988

河源
一群旅行者手执酒瓶伫立望天豪饮，随后
将空瓶猛力抛掷在脚底高迥的路。
一次准宗教祭仪。
一地碎片如同鳞甲而令男儿动容。
内陆漂起。

1988.12.12

THE LANTERN FESTIVAL

The colorful lanterns are piled up on the cold and lonely sea like flowers
blooming all night long
Time turns into endless moments like a drizzle urges Chinese bananas to
become mature

Cherishing green cypress grows moss, recalling the death of Sui Renshi,
the first fire-maker, drinking Biluochun Tea on snowing days,
all reveal the magic of life, so powerful, surprising, and mysterious.

February 21, 1989

元宵

寂冷如海上花灯堆放通宵达旦独自璀璨
时光如淅沥细雨催发芭蕉留下淅沥不尽的瞬刻

回味翠柏生苔燧人作古碧螺冰天映照白雪
生的妙谛力透纸背石破天惊直承众妙之门

1989.2.21

THE HARAKUTU CSATLE

The castle is the eternal and sentimental theme of predestination.

The mask of glory has gone down in the west as the warriors cry in the Warfield,

It is as dazzling as beeswax but eventually softens and goes away like dust.

No matter it is the sword, the bronze arrow, the ancestors' bone flute,

It is not allowed to resist the magic of solar radiation,

The Creator always uses this shining wreath picked from the East every day

To make fun of species coldly, which can make people shudder,

And to arouse people's natural awe and veneration,

To let the brothers stand in reverence and fear of being disrespected,

Which brings warmness like fragrant cypress showing its kindness,

To comfort the lonely soul and provoke people's endless thoughts.

The castle has become a furnace of ore sintered by years,

With dark smoke, so broken and trifling, scarred and battered,

The remaining mound is like a section of moult left by a divine dragon always in the company of shepherds.

In autumn, grass named the tongues of wolves grows crazily all over the slope.

In the chilly frost and wind, they show their blood color by turns.

The cold and changeable sun has burned the skin and flesh of tourists visiting the ancient castle.

The slight noise in the mountains is like a shadow suddenly thickened,

It's like bats swarming from overseas

It's like the pressure of the soul itself.

哈拉库图

城堡，宿命永恒不变的感伤主题，
光荣的面具已随武士的呐喊西沉，
如同蜂蜡般炫目，而终软化，粉尘一般流失。
无论利剑，无论铜矢，无论先人的骨笛
都不容抗御日轮辐射的魔法，
造物总以这灼灼的、每日采自东方的花冠
冷眼嘲弄万类，可不寒而栗，
而唤醒世人天性敬畏的情感，
让思图妄动的手足虔诚肃立而惧于非礼，
而有一缕温馨袭来如柏木的清香呈示善的氛围，
按摩孤寂的灵魂，予人无限幽远的思绪。

城堡，这是岁月烧结的一炉矿石，
带着黯淡的烟色，残破委琐，千疮百孔，
滞留土丘如神龙皲缩的一段蜕皮在荒草
常与牧羊人为伴。
是在秋季，满坡疯长的狼舌头
在霜风料峭中先后吐露出血色，
太阳奇冷莫测已灼痛访古旅游者的细皮嫩肉，
山野细微的嚣声如同阴影骤然浓重，
好像自境外起飞成群袭来的蝙蝠
好像灵魂自身的压力。

Under the slope of the village, a line of elderly people leaning against the wall and sitting on the ground
Remain in the sunset for their sunbath,
Their faces seem to hang some transcendental mucus.
Until some Muslims come and sell kiln goods again after they repair wooden wheeled carts.
They wade across the brook beside the village and disappear in the mist outside the village.
No one in the world can tell me about the castle of Harakutu.
Because the burden of memory is inherently deep, and
Human beings are used to forgetting.
Human beings, like any animal, are accustomed to seeking advantages and avoiding disadvantages.
They follow the principle of happiness.

Some villagers guide me and say: In fact, history is history, unchanged.
That is the winding canal on the mountain we excavated when we were young. It is still in the old place.
It decays like an old infertile maid.
That canal has no water to flow.

坡底村巷，一列倚在墙垣席地端坐的老人
仍留在夕阳的余烬曝晒，
面部似挂有某种超验的黏液。
直到贩卖窑货的穆斯林商旅终于重新吆喝起修讫的木轮车，
蹚过村边小溪的过水路面隐没在村外雾霭，
没有一个世人能够向我讲述哈拉库图城堡。
记忆的负重先天深沉。
人类习惯遗忘。
人类与任何动物无别而习于趋利避害。
而遵循快乐原则。

乡亲指给我说：其实历史就是历史啊，
我们年轻时挖掘的盘山水渠还在老地方，
衰朽如一个永远不得生育的老处女。
那是一条不曾走水的水渠。

But Halakutu Castle had witnessed a vivid, colorful life.

I am sure that no ancient person has fewer tears than today,

No ancient people have more joy than today.

At that time, the ancients praised those heroes who were outstanding in skill and brave on battlefields.

At that time, the drunken people who praised many invincible people were all heroes. I

have read some fragments from the remained annals of Halakutu as the following:

... Halakutu Castle was an important hub for businessmen,

In ancient times, a brigade of soldiers died on the battlefield when they departed from the west gate with no survivors!

Since then, the west gate was closed to commemorate them, and the east gate was opened only.

Ah, you blow a pottery Xun, an ancient egg-shaped holed wind instrument made in your hometown,

To play a folk song, sadly

telling the story about Han Dundun, a plump girl.

To you, she is your great cause of immortality?

Ah, the singer! Tell us why she is so cute and named Han Dundun?

You reply that no one can tell the answer.

Han Dundun, why do people call her Han Dundun? The answer is hard to tell...

The meaning of Han Dundun is hard to tell...hard to tell...hard to tell...

Ah, is your pottery Xun made in your hometown playing

an ode to the unsolved knot of human nature since ancient times?

但是哈拉库图城堡有过鲜活的人生。
我确信没有一个古人的眼泪比今人更少，
也没有一个古人的欢乐比今人更多。
那时古人称颂技勇超群而摧锋陷阵者皆曰好汉。
那时称颂海量无敌而一醉方休的酒徒皆是壮士。我
正是从哈拉库图城纪残编读到如下章句：
……哈拉库图城堡为行商往来之要区，
古昔有兵一旅自西门出征殁于阵无一生还者
哀壮士不归从此西门雍闭不开仅辟东门……

啊，你被故土捏制的陶埙
又在那里哇哇呜地吹奏着一个
关于憨墩墩的故事了。
唯有你的憨墩墩才是不朽的大事业么？
啊，歌人，憨墩墩的她哩为何唤作憨墩墩哩？
你回答说那是谁也说不清道不明的事哩，
憨墩墩嘛至于憨墩墩嘛……那意思深着……
憨墩墩那意思深着……深着……深着……
啊，你被故土捏制的陶埙莫不是在奏着一个
从古到今谁也不曾解开的人性死结？

Time is the perplexing magic.

I feel that a single day in childhood was as long as centuries.

I feel that the late autumn in adulthood is like an unfulfilled social drink.

It seems to me that everything far away happened yesterday.

And life is fragile in coming and going.

Every time I climb up a ladder to the mountain, I will experience loss again.

It's raining. I still go back to a villager's old wooden hut,

The host asks me to sit on a heatable brick bed with my legs crossed and opens the carved window.

He says that no craftsman could carve such a beautiful lattice anymore.

He refuses to replace it with a new glass window.

He invites me to watch his white horse across the rain curtain.

That is his white horse.

A waning moon is rising above the saddle on the horseback.

After the rain, a waning moon appears in the sky,

Casting light on the empty shell of the disillusionment of the ancient castle.

The white horse always shakes its tail.

The owner himself is sitting on a kang, the brick bed, with legs crossed and tasting tea too,

watching the white horse in the distant mountains striding

in a concentric circle forever,

Crying aloud into the sky forever.

Crying aloud into the sky forever.

时间啊，令人困惑的魔道，
我觉得儿时的一天漫长如绵绵几个世纪。
我觉得成人的暮秋似一次未尽快意的聚饮。
我仿佛觉得遥远的一切尚在昨日。
而生命脆薄本在转瞬即逝。
我每攀登一级山梯都要重历一次失落。

下雨了。我仍回到乡亲往昔的小木屋，
主人让我盘膝坐到炕头，为我撑开雕花窗棂。
他说再没有一个匠人造得出这样的雕花活计了
他执意不肯换装新式玻璃窗扇。
他让我隔着雨帘观赏远山他的一匹白马。
这是他的白马。
马的鞍背之上正升起一盏下弦月
雨后天幕正升起一盏下弦月，
映照古城楼幻灭的虚壳。
白马时时剪动尾翼。
主人自己就是这样盘膝坐在炕头品茶
一边观赏远山急急踏步的白马
永远地踏着一个同心圆，
永远地向空鸣嘶。
永远地向空鸣嘶。

The owner asked me to stay alone in this empty room that night,

He advised me to stop thinking about the castle

He said it was very dirty,

He said that the hole filled with pebbles had excavated many white bones.

He told me to rest early.

Before leaving, he was worried about whether I was lonely and scared at night.

He said that the grandmothers would be happy with my return.

At midnight, a Chausie broke into my hut and

caused a convulsive whirlwind.

When the owner got up early and found that the cat had taken the butter on the incense table.

The owner explained that the grandmothers must have been happy to see me back last night.

Ah, all the mysterious emotions had already existed in the past generations.

However, the ancient books were scattered, and the official documents were burned. Every day they could be destroyed in the world.

Imagining how hard the living Buddhas found their preaching places and how witch rituals were held to please gods after they had travelled thousands of miles in the wildland.

Imagining how the prince and his people wore animal hides, fought with their bowshots on horseback, and built their tents and blockages on the hills.

Imagining how to display the Eight Diagrams like ancient sage with gongs, drums, flutes, pipes, simple board, and wooden fish and how the scholar's servant recited the chapter of Positioning Heaven and Earth in I Ching (*The Book of Changes*).

这一晚夕主人让我独自留宿在这间空屋，
他劝我不要再寻思城堡的事
他说那里很脏很脏很脏，
他说那处填满卵石的坑穴刨出过许多白骨。
他让我早些安歇。
临别却又担心无人与我伴睡是否害怕。
他说奶奶们会因我的归来而高兴。
子夜，一头狮子猫闯入我的枕席
刮起了一阵痉挛的旋风。
早起，主人发觉供在香案的一方酥油已被叼失。
主人解释说奶奶们昨夜见我归来竟已如此高兴。

啊，情感的一切玄思妙想原就早都有过的了。
唯古卷散轶，案牍焚如，每日几成绝响。
想那活佛驻锡，巫祝娱神，行空荒之地千里。
想那王子百姓衣皮引弓之民驰骋凭陵插帐筑墩。
想那金鼓笛管简板木鱼布先王八卦书童诵《易经·天地定位》之章。

Imagining how emperors, gentry and people used different canopies, covers and banners on the roads.

Imagining how women on the mountains gathered cow milk into their nine pails to worship Buddha.

All the mysterious thoughts of emotion have already been experienced.

Only substances are decayed, and the fire of desires is still blazing.

There is no difference between the ancient and the modern. There is no difference between the times and against them.

All faces are just yesterday's ones.

All time is just the original one.

The feverish forehead is like a golden plate ready to collect nectar.

Look up to that star of hope, and my expectation is like a drop of grapes.

Ah, the beauty of the past, then

Her thick braided hair was as black as an untied cable rope

Overflowing with the smell of sulfur baked by the golden sun of Halakutu.

Her youth's intoxication was like a young bird's coyness when it first saw the sunshine. Where to find it again?

Do human beings enjoy their youth only once in their life?

I remember seeing a girl holding her flowers

to the wedding bed and then learning the outcome of the later generations.

My old friend told me her eldest child was too sick to get up.

Her youngest son became deaf after taking medicine by mistake.

Her lame husband was washed down by the mountain torrent and lost one of his arms.

想那锦盖幡幛绅民皇皇。
想那驻牧山头的妇人聚牛乳九筲礼佛。
情感的一切玄思妙想原就早都有过的了。
衰亡的只有物质，欲望之火却仍自炽烈。
无所谓今古。无所谓趋时。
所有的面孔都只是昨日的面孔。
所有的时间都只是原有的时间。
被烧得高热的额头如一只承接甘露的黄金盘，
仰望那一颗希望之星，
期待如一滴欲坠的葡萄。

啊，昔日的美人，那时
她的浓浓的辫发乌亮油黑如一部解开的缆索
流溢着哈拉库图金太阳炙烤的硫磺气味，
而那青春的醉意是一雏鸟初识阳光时眉眼迷离的娇羞，而今安在？
青春予人享有仅是一次性的权利？
我记得先是看见一个女孩擎举着自己的花朵
走向婚寝，而后得知了那一世代相传的结局。
故人向我告知她的大孩子原已一病不起。
小儿子服药耳聋成了哑人。
瘸腿的丈夫被山洪冲倒从此胳臂残缺不全。

My friend said that she often suffered from epilepsy and bit the tip of her
tongue without consciousness.

Her beautiful face was gone, just like the flower bed in spring withers in
an instant?

If the truth of time is just a mental image of illusory,

can the bleak evening at Halakutu differ from others?

Everything is so lonely,

Have you ever seen a red sky burned by fire?

Have you ever seen a sleepless night fighting for steel production?

Have you ever seen a beautiful bride like a flower?

Have you ever seen the eagle of Halakutu?

Have you ever seen a real poet who was exiled to the frontier?

He was so lonely, lonely, lonely,

Like a buzzing bee struggling between loneliness and noise.

Fate and opportunity were equally unreasonable.

At noon, I met the hearse for a young woman's funeral.

An old drummer leaned out of the hearse's door and window,

playing sad suona music in full strength

His voice was as loud as a cold woman in red,

delivering a transcendental beauty.

I followed the hearse to her cemetery

I heard blood dripping from my heart all the way.

故人说她常犯癫痫而咬碎舌尖。
美丽的容颜只是春日的花圃顷刻即会凋敝？
如果时间的真实只是虚幻的心像，
哈拉库图萧瑟的黄昏还会可能与众不同？
一切都是这样的寂寞啊，
果真有过被火焰烤红的天空？
果真有过为钢铁而鏖战的不眠之夜？
果真有过如花的喜娘？
果真有过哈拉库图之鹰？
果真有过流寓边关的诗人？
是这样的寂寞啊寂寞啊寂寞啊，
像一只嗡嗡飞远的蜜蜂，寂寞与喧哗同样真实。
而命运的汰选与机会同样不可理喻。
正午，我与为一少妇出殡的灵车邂逅。
年老的吹鼓手将腰身探出驾驶室门窗，
可着劲儿吹奏一支凄绝哀婉的唢呐曲牌，
音调高亢如红装女子一身寒气闪烁，
传送了一种超然的美丽。
我跟随灵车向墓地缓行
我听见心尖滴血暗暗洒满一路。

No one feels lonely and frustrated if he has never gone through the ups and downs in life.

No fallen warrior is not instantly shrunk and looks like a dwarf.

Does our death purify our life?

Autumn, autumn, autumn...

The shining horn of the icy mountain has given out a sense of awe and ruthlessness.

Broad-leaved trees shook off their leaves and floated them in the rainwater last night.

The remained leaves looked like beautiful eyes and brought people comfort and warmth.

They showed their attitude towards life with unspoken words, being natural and lofty.

Who was screaming and fighting against their predestination on the wasteland?

The wooden wheeled carts selling kiln goods had gone farther and farther.

The ruins of Halakutu had finally become tired.

But in the eyes of climbers, the hilltop had been spliced by wheat and golden brassica.

At that moment, the hilltop turned bigger and bigger, like a head of an ancient warrior.

Her green broom-shaded eyebrows stirred a clamor of tides.

He was horrified by his sudden discovery in front of him as if he had

a heart attack! He wondered why the translation of Halakutu was the Black Lama?

Was our history always called a heroic play of jests?

October 9-24, 1989,

on the way back from the pasture of Riyue Mountain

没有一个历尽沧桑者不曾有落寞的挫折感。
没有一个倒毙的猛士不是顷刻萎缩形同侏儒。
死亡终是对生的净化？
秋天啊，秋天啊，秋天啊……
高山冰凌闪烁的射角已透出肃杀之气，
阔叶林木扬落残叶任其铺满咋夜的雨水，
唯此眉眼似的残叶还约可予人一派蕴藉的温情，
以不言之言刻意领悟存在，乘化淡远。
竟又是谁在大荒熹微之中嗷声舒啸抵牾宿命？
贩卖窑货的木轮车队已愈去愈加迢遥。
哈拉库图城墟也终于疲惫了。
而在登山者眼底被麦季与金色芸薹垄亩拼接的
山垴此刻赫然膨大如一古代武士的首级，
绿色帚眉掀起一片隐隐潮动的嚣声。
他为眼前这一突然发现而震悚觉心力衰竭顿生
恐惧。他不解哈拉库图的译意何以是黑喇嘛。
历史啊总也意味着一部不无谐戏的英雄剧？

　　　　　　　　1989.10.9—24 于日月山牧地来归

MY VISITS FROM CITY TO CITY WITH A CAP ON

From city to city
I salute the cities along the way with my shovel-shaped cap
and beard. Fastening my backpack
I have joined the mighty afternoon tide of people in the S City.

I don't know where the sun rises and where it sets.
I don't know where the wind comes from.
But I know the land where lights on fishing boats and keels develop.
The dark river is covered fully with colorful freighters,
However, the ancient wells inlaid in the old streets have lost their vitality
The clean stinkpots are lined with stone railings, which look like ancient
wine urns.
The heat is steaming in my long hair.
I can experience life's passion better than a woman with long hair.

I began to look for a small lane.
Looking for a poet buried by time.
He deduces eight Diagrams to foresee his fate and dig a river of gold in
the humble house.

头戴便帽从城市到城市的造访

从城市到城市
我以铲形的便帽向着沿途的城市致意，
而不只以胡须。系好背囊
我已加入 S 市浩荡的午潮了。

不知太阳从何处升起又向何处降落。
不知风从何方吹来。
但我知道渔火与龙骨发育的土地，
黝黑的河流盖满色彩斑斓的货船了，
而老街镶嵌的古井意兴阑珊，那里
涮净的马桶排立石栏形如古风淳朴的酒罍。
暑气在我的长发云蒸了。
我比长发女人更能体验日子的热烈。

我开始寻找一条小小的弄堂。
寻找一位被岁月埋没的诗人。
他在蜗居推演八卦研讨命运开凿淘金之河。

No guide in the world can point out his door number for me.

They don't like my cap. People here don't remember the cap fashion.

But where has the generation gone who enjoy wearing their caps?

I felt a kind of haggard in my eyes.

My cap becomes suddenly old too.

From a face mask to a masked face,

From a karst house to a house karst,

we know the hard journey is the psychological one.

I am attracted to landscapes' advertisements and to advertised landscapes.

As a routine, the gardener still decorates his passionless flower basket

with no other distractions, and he finds nothing shines on the stamens.

They don't like my cap.

Now I am fatigued again in a passionless life.

Is there a flesh and blood relationship between gardeners, cities and caps?

I guess this city must discriminate against hats.

Who can remember the Turkish poem "On the Beanie and the Woven
Hat"?

Who can remember the poet Nazim Hikmet wearing a worker's cap six
days a week, walking Proudly on the streets of Turkish cities?

The poet dreamed that he would own 20 million woolen hats.

It was an optimistic era that treasured the corolla cap-like life.

Who can remember his generation of innocent and lovely old people?

这个世界再没有向导能够为我指明这块门牌了。
他们不喜欢我的便帽。这里不记得便帽。
然而那头戴便帽的一代已去往何处？
感觉眼中升起一种憔悴。
我的便帽也蓦然衰老了。
从脸孔似的面具直到面具似的脸孔，
从岩溶似的屋宇直到屋宇似的岩溶，
艰难的跋涉属于心理的跋涉了。
我从风景似的广告走向广告似的风景，
花匠仍以例行剪修着每日的缺少激情的花篮，
无意旁骛。没有什么还会在花蕊上闪耀了。
他们不喜欢我的便帽。

现在我重新体验缺少激情的生活的劳累了。
难道花匠、城市与便帽之间会有一种血肉联系？
我猜想这定然是一座歧视帽子的城市了。
那么谁还记得土耳其诗篇《关于便帽和呢帽》？
那么谁还记得诗人希克梅特每周六天头戴工人便帽
骄傲地走向土耳其城市大街？
诗人梦想着自己将占有两千万顶呢帽。
那是一个护卫花冠如同生命的乐观时代。
那么谁还记得有过一代纯真而可爱的遗老？

I think of a group of young people who gave a farewell dinner to their friend who planned to go to the frontier.

The traveler was silent, the giver was speechless, and they could not enjoy drinking and eating with cups and chopsticks.

During the dinner, they felt bleak that their friend would not return from the western frontier.

It seemed I was the hero who decided to go west without returning.

At that time, the hermit I was looking for sent his welcome message to me by electric sound.

He led me through the maze of streets

and opened his iron security door for me, then the second plank door for me to enter his house.

I asked if he felt pitiful for my cap.

He unreservedly praised my cap and my wild

hairstyle and beard. We laughed together, removed our shoes and walked into the inner hall.

This was a small house cleverly hidden and well-decorated by the owner.

His wife had put bowls of sweet soup on the table.

In the evening, there was a salon like a gathering of poets.

Soon they all came to this study one after another.

I felt the joy of entering the city from the poets' handshakes.

So I often paid them my tribute with my shovel-shaped cap.

I told them the story of caps.

They said Neruda, Blok, Mayakovsky, Lorca... Whitman loved caps too.

Of course, Ah Loong or S. M. also loved to wear caps...

我想起一群青年为矢志远投边荒的朋友饯行，
行者噤声，送者失语，举觞投箸不能尽，
席间有着萧萧易水的寒凉。
我恍若自己就是那位决计西行不复的壮士了。
而那时我寻觅的隐士以电声向我传送他的歌吟了。
他引领我穿过迷宫似的街区，
为我打开铁栅防盗门，再打开二道板门。
我探询主人会不会因为我的便帽而觉遗憾。
他全无保留地赞美我的便帽并称誉我狂放的
发式及胡须。我们同声大笑脱掉鞋履步入内厅。
这是一间被主人精巧藏匿着的蜗居。
他的夫人已将甜羹一碗一碗盛放桌面了。
是晚有一次沙龙式的诗人聚会。
不久他们都陆续光临这间书斋。
从诗人的握手我才真正觉出进入城市的快乐了。
于是我以铲形的便帽频频致意。
我讲给他们便帽的故事。
他们说那时还有聂鲁达、勃洛克、马雅可夫斯基、洛尔伽……惠
特曼。
当然还应该有 S. M. 阿垅……

Scholar W from A country turned his Lenin-style coconut-shaped head
and talked about the popularity of Hikmate on the other side of the
Pacific Ocean, his North American continent.
And I interjected that as early as the 1950s, we had witnessed the
popularity of Hikmate in China.
The only generation left who worshiped Hikmet is us, the only one.
There might not be a more memorable conversation to be recorded under
the sky.

From one city to another,
I insist on saying goodbye to the cities along the way with my shovel-
shaped cap.
What else can we show our noble civilian spirit?
The flags of different businesses flutter freely in the night wind.
The metal flag posts in Fountain Square echo with their sharp hum.
This reminds me of recalling the cold wind in the west desert,
and my beard, as an evergreen plant, has fallen asleep on the rolling
wheels.

July 22, 1990

A 国学者 W 侧转他那列宁式的椰果似的脑颅，
讲说彼岸他的北美大陆正在兴起希克梅特热。
而我插言说早在五十年代我们就已热过了。
硕果仅存的一代只是唯一的我们。
苍穹之下未必还有比这更值得一记的恳谈了。

从城市到城市
我坚持以我铲形的便帽向着沿途的城市辞别。
除此而外还能以何物展示我们高贵的平民精神？
习习夜风中商界林立的旗帜潇洒地飘展了，
喷泉广场的金属旗柱以峻急的嗡鸣竞相呼应，
我记起西部荒漠疾风催生时的凛冽了。
而我的胡须作为不凋的草木已在车轮摇滚中进入梦乡。

1990.7.22

VIRGINS

I take a hen's boiled egg from an earthen pot, strip off the shell, and the egg white protein looks like beautiful jade. I am secretly excited because I suddenly think of youth: Yes, it looks like a virgin, plump and smooth-skinned. It looks like a virgin, pure and clean. It looks like a virgin, tender and fresh. Therefore, does the youth's body have to take heaven and earth's essence to resist aging? Ah, it is really a symbol of irony. Only crazy people, like Van Gogh and Nietzsche, Jie Yu, succeed in resisting their aging because they are natural and unrestrained. They endure their thoughts squeezed and pressed, and their spiritual fruits are materialized like hens' boiled eggs. Is it a hatred for their survival? Is it feedback to their beloved? But their self-completed destruction also results from the fire of passion, and how does the fire become aging? How shocking it is when you realize the youth is self-destroyed.

January 2 to 3, 1991

处子

我自瓦罐取来煮熟的鸡卵，揭去拍打松软的壳衣，凝冻如玉的蛋白体就完整地裸现眼底了。我暗自激动，因为那时我忽有青春之思：——是啊，这真是处子一样的丰润啊。这真是处子一样的纯净啊。这真是处子一样的娇嫩而鲜美啊。因此，青春的胴体才要殚思极虑调摄天地之精以抗拒衰老的迫近？……啊，真是嘲讽的象征呀，被认作成功地却拒了衰老者唯有狂士，唯有凡高、尼采，唯有接舆而歌者流不羁的幽灵。忍受着自己思想之挤压、煎逼的精神果实，终于如沸煮后的鸡卵冷却剥离物化。是对于生存的憎恨？是对于所爱之反哺？但那一自我完成的毁灭也属于热情之火，而火又如何衰老？毁灭其于青春的寓意又是如何地让人深感愕然啊。

1991.1.2—3

A DROP OF HERO'S TEARS

Here is a drop of the hero's tears.

A great wizard utters a curse: It is a fatal blow. He will die.

Yes, a bone thorn from his wound is the venomous tooth of a snake.

His blood is surging from the wound. But he is still alive. It seems a shame for him to be alive.

Alas! Fate always makes some people restless all their lives.

Fate makes them bleed and never die, making them braver and braver after more frustration.

The significance of the life purpose is not important, but the process of life is more important.

Is that the charm of our daily life?

June 30, 1992

一滴英雄泪

一滴英雄泪。
大巫师诅咒了：那是致命的一击。他将死。
不错，从伤口钳出的骨刺确属蛇的毒牙。
血流汹涌。但人还活着。说也惭愧竟还活着。
命运啊，你总让一部分人终身不得安宁，
让他们流血不死，然后又让他们愈挫愈奋。
目的的意义似乎并不重要而贵在过程显示。
日子就是这样的魅力么？

1992.6.30

TO XIUHUANG

Dear Huang: I never realize that I love you so much.

Does too much love from me make you feel so tired?

Does it make you think lions' love is also very beautiful?

I am tired too. I understand the severe situation, I have my secret pain.

But I will become vulgar again if I lose your love.

My body is full of scars; my eyes are a blur and as blue as a pastoral.

You have been showered with my hurt several times. You must have been bitterly disappointed with me.

You have smoothed my eyebrow knot with your tenderness.

You tell me kissing can make us more beautiful.

I sit up again and find the earth is ablaze with lights, like a candle for ritual sacrifice.

It seems that we are the subjects of sacrifice,

and we feel private that we have arrogated a ritual solemnness.

Yes, maybe I will die in peace and in silence.

I can get my last consolation if I choose to die.

Love is like two windows facing each other at both ends of a lane, as innocent as a pastoral life.

When one has no intention to explain to the other, their expectation is also futile.

I have so many worries and dare not to appear in the dead city like a desert.

致修篁

篁：我从来不曾这么爱，
所以你才觉得这爱使你活得很累么？
所以你才称狮子的爱情原也很美么？
我亦劳乏，感受严峻，别有隐痛，
但若失去你的爱我将重归粗俗。
我百创一身，幽幽目光牧歌般忧郁，
将你几番淋透。你已不胜寒。
你以温心为我抚平眉结了，
告诉我亲吻可以美容。
我复坐起，大地灯火澎湃，恍若蜡炬祭仪，
恍若我俩就是受祭的主体，
私心觉着僭领了一份祭仪的肃穆。
是的，也许我会宁静地走向寂灭，
如若死亡选择才是我最后可获的慰藉。
爱，是间巷两端相望默契的窗牖，田园般真纯，
当一方示意无心解语，期待也是徒劳。
我已有了诸多不安，惧现沙漠的死城。

Therefore, I unbraid your hair and embrace you with my whole body.

I seem to hold you as a magic bird that will fly away anytime.

I make my salute to your deep-lake eye sockets with my juicy eyes.

My gaze will overflow with the beauty of the setting sun after many years.

You, my dear Huang: We know there will be many swamps and deep valleys in the future.

Why do we rush to know each other?

Since then, I have been very moody, fickle, haggard, and stubborn.

Please forgive me for kidnapping you with my love: I have become a tyrant.

I have turned such a tyrant only.

1997.7.27 draft
1992.9.21 revised

因此我为你解开发辫周身拥抱你，
如同强挽着一头会随时飞遁的神鸟，
而用我多汁的注目礼向着你深湖似的眼窝倾泻，
直到要漫过岁月久远之后斜阳的美丽。
你啊，篁：既知前途尚多大泽深谷，
为何我们又要匆匆急于相识？
从此我忧喜无常，为你变得如此憔悴而玩劣。
啊，原谅我欲以爱心将你裹挟了：是这样的暴君。
仅只是这样的暴君。

　　　　　　　　　　1992.7.27 初稿，9.21 改定

DON QUIXOTE'S LEGION IS STILL ADVANCING

In the East

Don Quixote's legion is parading.

Don Quixote has become a laughing stock, and his clan is prosperous.

The drums, pipes and bugles are played together.

Skinny horses, short donkeys and camels march forward side by side in a line.

Don Quixote never doubts how long his spearhead will last for long.

He never believes the knight's flag will fall.

He refuses to be enlightened in this world.

But I heard the singing like that, knocking at the door.

(His battle song goes like this: Ah, we harvest, we grind, we hoe.

... Ah, we fly, we bring incense, we burn ourselves.

We will live again like a phoenix does after its burning.)

堂·吉诃德军团还在前进

东方
堂·吉诃德军团的阅兵式。
予人笑柄的族类，生生不息的种姓。
架子鼓、笙篁和军号齐奏。
瘦马、矮驴同骆驼排在一个队列齐头并进。
从不怀疑自己的镶枪头还能挺多久。
从不相信骑士的旗帜就此倒下。
拒绝醍醐灌顶。
但我听到那样的歌声剥啄剥啄，敲门敲门。
（是这样唱着：啊，我们收割，我们打碾，我们锄禾。
……啊，我们飞呀飞呀，我们衔来香木，我们自焚，
我们凤凰再生。……）

Don Quixote's legion starts from the ancient tombs, and they march forward with a full load.

They experienced many failures and records of losing armor and spears on their way.

Its immortality lies in the purity of its spiritual value.

The word, never, is not the worst setback, but it is always the most serious moment.

Don Quixote packs some clothes, wears rags and drives a firewood cart to start their conquering.

A line of his fatigue people and skinny horses walk towards the explosion of the setting sun.

After so many bloody fights and glories, their inverted images or shadows are spread out from their feet.

They stretch across the gravel field and stand as straight as a clump of Suoyang, a herb medicine —

The wild horses intersect with mosquitoes and dragons, producing bulbs and plants.

What a tragedy! There is no one left uncultivated.

Don Quixote's legion has struggled against the windmills in the world.

They also have challenged so many wine vessels.

They proceed without hesitation to retake the chastity of the kidnapped virgins and regain the honor of the trampled noble women.

They have borne all the bitterness of beating and suffered all satires.

The young Princess Dulcinea will never grow up as his lover.

He will never realize this truth until death - he refuses to follow evil words.

He remains immature all his life. His soul suffers eternally.

He always bears the burden of history.

从远古的墓茔开拔，满负荷前进，
一路狼狈尽是丢盔卸甲的纪录。
不朽的是精神价值的纯粹。
永远不是最坏的挫折，但永远是最严重的关头。
打点行装身披破衣驾着柴车去开启山林。
鸠形鹄面行吟泽边一行人马走向落日之爆炸。
被血光辉煌的倒影从他们足下铺陈而去，
曳过砾原，直与那一片丛生的锁阳 ——
野马与蚊龙嬉戏遗精入地而生的鳞茎植群相交。
悲壮啊，竟没有一个落荒者。

冥冥天地间有过无尽的与风车的搏斗。
有过无尽的向酒罍的挑战。
为夺回被劫持的处女的贞洁及贵妇人被践踏的荣誉义无反顾。
吃尽皮肉之苦，遭到满堂哄笑。
少女杜尔西内亚公主永远长不大的情人，
永远的至死不悟 —— 拒绝妖言。
永远的不成熟。永远的灵魂受难。
永远的背负历史的包袱。

The dinner will be over, and the benefactor will leave the table,

Don Quixote and his heroes are not embarrassed.

But this is the most critical moment for them.

How can they defeat the fiery mouths of modern gluttonous beasts?

They ignore the temptations and use their spears to support their tents.

They start a campfire with heart oil and sit cross-legged for meditation.

They call themselves Eastern Rangers, full of Utopian illusion and devote themselves to their noble cause.

This is their final struggle. But in the name of omnipotence, the magic of omnipotence makes a comeback.

The wind is rustling, and the water is cold. It is time for the heroes to start their conquer journey. The Yishui River is behind them.

We are devout. We pursue our dreams. We are vegetarians.

We know we can't achieve our goals, and we know we are homeless dogs.

What a tragedy! There is no one left uncultivated.

What a tragedy! For sure, there is no one left uncultivated.

August 5, 1993

饭局将撤，施主少陪，
堂·吉诃德好汉们无心尴尬。
但这是最最严重的关头，
匹夫之勇又如何战胜现代饕餮兽吐火的焰口？
无视形而下的诱惑，用长矛撑起帐幄，
以心油燃起营火，盘膝打坐。
东方游侠，满怀乌托邦的幻觉，以献身者自命。
这是最后的斗争。但是万能的魔法又以万能的名义卷土重来。

风萧萧兮易水寒。背后就是易水。
我们虔敬。我们追求。我们素餐。
我们知其不可而为之，累累若丧家之狗。
悲壮啊，竟没有一个落荒者。
悲壮啊，实不能有一个落荒者。

1993.8.5

THE STREET GUARD

Infinite foam, night foam, and night filters.

A semi-insomniac is the one between the healthy and the impure.

He will drift among the bubble of dreams, going in and out of dreams.

The semi-insomniac on the street becomes a guard of the street.

The drunkard's voice is dull and boring.

It tears people's hearts. Who can preach benevolence, courtesy and justice to him?

Later, a person returning home at night beats an iron door.

Finally, a suona player performs professionally and accompanies the hearse toward the western paradise.

The sleeping baby lies in the cradle to savor the joy of his past life.

The semi-insomniac is the most unfortunate; his nightmares

are all repeated suffering.

But the dawn is like a clean stream flowing through these dreams.

The dark blue of rock roll is as authentic as the steel coating.

All monsters and devils will not be bothered for the time being.

August 18, 1993

大街看守

无穷的泡沫，夜的泡沫，夜的过滤器。
半失眠者介于健康与不净之间，
在梦的泡沫中浮沉，梦出梦入。
街边的半失眠者顺理成章地成了大街的看守。

寡淡乏味，醉鬼们的歌喉
撕扯着人心，谁能对他们说教仁爱礼义？
一会儿是夜归人狠揍一扇铁门。
唢呐终于吹得天花乱坠，陪送灵车赶往西天。
安寝的婴儿躺卧在摇篮回味前世的欢乐。
只有半失眠者最为不幸，他的噩梦
通通是其永劫回归的人生。
但黎明已像清澈的溪流贯注其间，
摇滚的幽蓝像钢材的镀层真实可信，
一切的魑魅魍魉暂时不复困扰。

1993.8.18

THE HUMORIST DIED
(A SUDDEN FEELING COMES WITH NO REASON)

The last master of humor has died, and this world has no humor.

A master of humor feels pain in his heart, and he disdains any impromptu comic gestures and remarks. He disdains to be funny. Although he is not equal to satire, he is not only humorous.

A master of humor with painful essence is the self-presence that ordinary people can be proud of. It is the self-comfort that common people can obtain. It is another "self" that common people are good at explaining.

A serious humorist has died, and another one will never be reincarnated for us. In the distress that the Ebola virus, mad cow virus, HIV, human smuggling, death row prisoners, conspiracy, etc., have threatened us one after another, there will not be a second master of humor who will come to accept our worship and pray for us.

However, many impostors, bad imitators and clowns still live by fishing for fame.

Only the so-called laughter manufacturing industry is left.

Therefore, he is the last dead humorist.

The world has lost the Holy Grail and the sword.

The dried human umbilical cord no longer secretes healthy nutrients for the brain.

March 25, 1996

幽默大师死去
（一次蓦然袭来的心潮）

最后一个幽默大师已经死了，这世界再也不存在幽默。

一个本质痛苦的幽默大师，不屑于插科打诨。不屑于滑稽。他虽不等同于讽刺，但也不仅仅只是幽默。

一个本质痛苦的幽默大师，是庶民可引以为荣的自我存在。是庶民可借以获得的自我安慰。是庶民善作解语的另一个"自我"。

一个本质严肃的幽默大师已经死了，再不会有第二个为我们转世再生。在埃博拉病毒、疯牛病毒、艾滋病毒……人口走私、死囚……阴谋……等等相继威胁我们的苦闷中，不会有第二个幽默大师临世接受我们膜拜并替我们摩顶祈福。

但是，世上仍不乏冒名的僭越者、拙劣的效颦者及沽名钓誉赖以为生的小丑。

只剩下了所谓笑的制造行业。

因之，他是最后一个死去的幽默大师。

这世界失去了圣杯，也同时失去了宝剑。

干枯了的人类脐带不再分泌健脑的营养素。

1996. 3.25

TO A PAIR OF PETITE PAINTED POTTERY POTS IN THE PRE-HISTORY

Ah, free spirits, when will you be with your sisters in distress
and fall into the slave market together as auctioned in public.
It seems that someone pokes the wound and then suddenly sprinkles a
handful of salt particles,
I hear the man cheering the long life of private ownership in the name of
freedom.

You, the most beautiful symbols, have the smell of smoke in the pre-
history,
Laying out a thin layer of frost powder from ancient agricultural
civilization on the sweaty skin.
The breath that has doubled my extension leads to the fetal sound of
history's annihilation,
feeling a humanistic flower emerging with the dewy dawn.

Please forgive me for redeeming and bringing you back to my desk.
At that moment, I suddenly realized that your arms were on your hips,
just like the beautiful ladies in the ochre dress in the street dance team,
who can continue to rehearse your beautiful idyllic songs at any time.

But why? Whenever I glance at it after work,
I always see you rush back to a static dance in panic.
I will never be able to integrate with you in another time and space.
I sign that the source of life is irreversibly hidden in the eternal solar
eclipse.

March 26, 1998

致史前期一对娇小的彩陶罐

啊，自由的精灵，你们何时与遭难的姐妹
一同落入奴隶市场的围栏被当众标价拍卖。
好像由人捅开伤口再陡然撒上一把盐粒，
我听见那人正借自由之名欢呼私有制万岁。

你们，绝美的象征，秘藏史前期熏烟之气息，
如微汗沁出肤体敷一层远古农耕文明的薄霜粉，
使我加倍延伸的呼吸通向了历史湮灭的胎音，
感受一株人文花朵伴随曙光初露破土而出。

啊，请原谅孤处的我将你们赎身接到我的案头。
那刻我忽有所感悟，发现你们双臂支在腰臀，
恰是陌上歌舞队里身着赭红裙裾的窈窕淑女，
可随时继续排练你们秀色可餐的田园之歌。

然而所为何来，每当工余我凝目投去一瞥，
总见你们惊慌中匆忙还原于一个静态的舞姿，
永远留下了我不能与彼一时空融合的苦闷，
感慨走来的源头不可逆转地深隐在终古的日食。

1998.3.26

ELEVEN RED ROSES

A coastal woman flew to the North Desert to visit a dying elder,
On parting, she presented the unfortunate friend with red roses.

Girl, why are there only eleven red roses?
The girl said this symbolized my respect for you and was full of my
heart.

One day later, the elderly's condition suddenly worsened.
The cunning god of death did not give the prey a moment to breathe.

Girl, since you left, I have felt hopeless.
Besides, the god of death said that he would give me rest as long as I
obeyed him.

My friend, my friend, you must stand firm.
When I departed from you, I said what I told you was true?

Girl, I am in great pain when I live every minute of my life.
Besides, the god of death said he would give me a long sleep if I obeyed
him.

一十一支红玫瑰

一位滨海女子飞往北漠看望一位垂死的长者，
临别将一束火红的玫瑰赠给这位不幸的朋友。

姑娘啊，火红的一束玫瑰为何端只一十一支，
姑娘说，这象征我对你的敬重原是一心一意。

一天过后长者的病情骤然恶化，
刁滑的死神不给猎物片刻喘息。

姑娘姑娘自你走后我就觉出求生无望，
何况死神说只要听话他就会给我安息。

我的朋友啊我的朋友你可要千万挺住，
我临别不是说嘱咐你的一切绝对真实？

姑娘姑娘我每存活一分钟都万分痛苦，
何况死神说只要听话他就会给我长眠。

My friend, my friend, you must stand firm.

You should understand how important you were in my eyes.

Girl, I might leave without telling you at any time.

Besides, the god of death said he did not treat me halfheartedly.

After three days, eleven red roses all lowered their heads in silence.

A coastal woman was weeping quietly for the elder in the North Desert.

March 15, 2000, on the sickbed

我的朋友啊我的朋友你可要千万挺住，
你应该明白你在我们眼中的重要位置。

姑娘姑娘我随时都将可能不告而辞，
何况死神说他待我也不是二意三心。

三天过后一十一支玫瑰全部垂首默立，
一位滨海女子为北漠长者在悄声饮泣。

　　　　　　　　2000. 3.15 于病榻

BAMBOO FLUTE IN FOREST

1. The Wheel

Alas, the decayed wheel...... Let it ignite our flaming campfire, and join us in passionate singing.

— The prospector says.

There is a broken wheel in the forest swamp

Warmly reflecting half a circle of turbid shadows

It seems to have some faded transient joy, never waking from the lucid dream

Allowing wildfire to jump over, frogs strike up

The fleet rolls by forest day and night

Dust floats on the long road day and night

However, it can no longer fall in love with the long way

Lying quietly, as if waiting for the owner of the accident...

林中试笛（二首）

1. 车轮

　　唉，这腐朽的车轮……就让它燃起我们熊熊的篝火，加入我们激昂的高歌吧。
　　—— 勘探者语

在林中沼泽里有一只残缺的车轮
暖洋洋地映着半圈浑浊的阴影
它似有旧日的春梦，常年不醒
任凭磷火跳越，蛙声喧腾

车队日夜从林边滚过
长路上日夜浮着烟尘
但是，它却再不能和长路热恋
静静地躺着，似乎在等着意外的主人……

2. The Wild Goral

Well, long-tailed gorals, one-to-one fighting, they seem not to hear us
singing...
  Please be gentle and hand me the shotgun, a delicious soup I will hunt.
  — The prospector said.

In the clearing forest land, a morning
A pair of grumpy gorals are fighting
Who knows how many rounds they fight
With horns against each other, they are about to light

What old grudge makes them forget the meadow
What old grudge makes them fight a battle
The stubborn forest wildness
The shotgun is aimed at their still-fighting heads

Summer 1957

2. 野羊

啊，好一对格斗的青羊，似乎没听见我们高唱……请轻点，递给
我猎枪，猎一顿美味的鲜汤。
——勘探者语

在晨光迷离的林中空地
一对暴躁的青羊在互相格杀
谁知它们角斗了多少个回合
犄角相抵，快要触出火花

是什么宿怨，使它们忘记了青草
是什么宿怨，使它们打起了血架
这林中固执的野性啊
当猎枪已对准头颅，它们还在厮打

1957 夏

THE MOON AND THE GIRL

Moon, moon
Hollow valley of youth

Girl, girl
Lead a horse and move

A long way, a long way
Dew white, maple red

Way long, way long
Mountain north is the sun

Bright moon, bright moon
Wildfire should boom

July 27, 1957

月亮与少女

月亮月亮
幽幽空谷

少女少女
挽马徐行

长路长路
丹枫白露

路长路长
阴山之阳

亮月亮月
野火摇曳

1957.7.27

TREKKING AT NIGHT IN WESTERN PLATEAU

Trekking at night in the western plateau
I never feel solitude.

— The low smoke
Is guarded by the shepherd dog.
There are smells of ripe soil.
Often, I see the precipice of the mountain
Open a window, like the night's
Small cherrylike mouth, going to tell me what,
But suddenly, silent again.
I assume it's the mother of baby
Lights the oil lamp on the windowsill,
Then suddenly blows out......

1961 draft

夜行在西部高原

夜行在西部高原
我从来不曾觉得孤独。

—— 低低的熏烟
被牧羊狗所看护。
有成熟的泥土的气味儿。
不时，我看见大山的绝壁
推开一扇窗洞，像夜的
樱桃小口，要对我说些什么，
蓦地又沉默不语了。
我猜想是乳儿的母亲
点燃窗台上的油灯，
过后又忽地吹灭了……

1961 初稿

I AM LYING. EXPLOIT ME!

I am lying. Exploit me! I am the wasteland

I am the rock stratum, the river bed... Come and exploit me! I will

give you the most luxurious, abundant and magical colors.

To store your nowhere-to-let-off energy: Now I am at your service; I would

give your rotating wheels a full pleasure.

While I have breathed and smiled contentedly,

Also, with throes.

February 1962

我躺着。开拓我吧!

我躺着。开拓我吧!我就是这荒土
我就是这岩层,这河床……开拓我吧!我将
给你最豪华、最繁富、最具魔力之色彩。
储存你那无可发泄的精力:请随意驰骋。我要
给你那旋动的车轮以充实的快感。
而我已满足地喘息、微笑
又不无阵痛。

1962.2

THE GOOD NIGHT

The exiled poet

Does the good night belong to you?

Does the night with the sweet new bride belong to you?

Do the night-flowing mountains, waves and midnight clock tower

belong to you? Does the night bring out flower buds under the moonlight

like a little swan slowly spreading wings belong to you?

No, there is no moonlight tonight, no flowers, no swans,

My fingers are tinged with the smell of rain and grass,

But even a rainy night like this totally belongs to you?

Yes, it totally belongs to me.

But don't think my love is covered with plaque,

I get nutrients from the air and calcium from the sun,

My mustache is as tough as the arrow feather,

But my love is as shy as the night.

Oh, my friend, you speak with me at night

Please pass me your fine and slim hands.

September 14, 1962 in Qilian Mountain

良宵

放逐的诗人啊
这良宵是属于你的吗？
这新嫁娘的柔情蜜意的夜是属于你的吗？
这在山岳、涛声和午夜钟楼流动的夜
是属于你的吗？这使月光下的花苞
如小天鹅徐徐展翅的夜是属于你的吗？
不，今夜没有月光，没有花朵，也没有天鹅，
我的手指染着细雨和青草气息，
但即使是这样的雨夜也完全是属于你的吗？
是的，全部属于我。
但不要以为我的爱情已生满菌斑，
我从空气摄取养料，经由阳光提取钙质，
我的须髭如同箭毛，
而我的爱情却如夜色一样羞涩。
啊，你自夜中与我对语的朋友
请递给我十指纤纤的你的素手。

1962.9.14 于祁连山

THE DEVOUT MONK IN RED

Red poplar -- the devout monk,
Wearing the fiery-red cassock of autumn,
Silently guarding the garden...

Am I the stand-still idol?
My life is the road beaten in wind and rain towards the long run.
I fell in love with a strong body, brain skull and hands used to holding
the sickle.
I get to learn history.
I go to consciously inspect the underground tomb,
My discovery is the terrible truth shining at every step.

You see my eyes turning to the sky, mature day by day,
Filled with mellow and juicy love.

October 13-15, 1962

这虔诚的红衣僧人

红杨树 —— 虔诚的僧人，
裹着秋日火红的红袈裟，
默守一方园囿……

我是那种呆立的偶像吗？
我的生命是在风雨吹打中奔行在长远的道路。
我爱上了强健的肉体，脑颅和握惯镰刀的手。
我去熟悉历史。
我自觉地去察视地下的墓穴，
发现可怕的真理在每一步闪光。

你看我转向蓝天的眼睛一天天成熟，
充盈着醇厚多汁的情爱。

1962.10.13—15

THE BEAUTY

Beside the fence, there stands a rural beauty.

She silently takes off her straw hat,

Holds in hand and plays it like a golden moon, as if deep in thought.

There, falling upon her bouncy breasts,

Two plaits as thick as the vine,

Glitter with greasy drooping light

Why am I so shy?

Why would I deny the sense of beauty in my heart?

When I'm used to giving a secret glimpse at her!

September 23, 1979

美人

篱笆旁，一个乡村的美人。
她默默地脱下草帽，
拿在手中，摆弄如一轮金月，若有所思。
那里，垂落在她弹性的胸脯，
两根藤萝般粗实的发辫，
闪着油腻欲滴的光……
为什么我要羞涩？
为什么要否认进入心中的美感？
却习惯于偷偷地斜睇！

1979.9.23

THE SHIP OF MERCY

1. Love and Death

Indeed, in the wrestle between good and evil
the propagation and reproduction of love
is older than death,

    and much braver!

Me, I am such a love letter in action

I do not understand oblivion.
I am not used to numbness.
I sometimes use my orchid-shaped fingers
Flick towards the empty space --
It hurts the echo.

However,
Just to listen to the news of losers again
About their defeat
I just played this
Music with the ancient theme?
In the wrestle between good and evil
the propagation and reproduction of love
is older than death,

    and much braver!

慈航

1. 爱与死

是的，在善恶的角力中
爱的繁衍与生殖
比死亡的戕残更古老、
　　更勇武百倍。

我，就是这样一部行动的情书

我不理解遗忘。
也不习惯麻木。
我不时展示状如兰花的五指
朝向空阔弹去 ——
触痛了的是回声。

然而，
只是为了再听一次失道者
败北的消息
我才拨动这支
命题古老的琴曲？
在善恶的角力中
爱的繁衍与生殖
比死亡的戕残更古老、
　　更勇武百倍。

2. The Wasteland in Memory

Taking off the crown of thorns

He comes from the wasteland,

Retakes his own destiny.

Looking over the wilderness

The meteorological post

With snow-white capital

Lying, an arrowhead is peacefully on its side

But,

In the immortal wasteland —

Immortal

The lonely marmot behind the loose mounds

Raises its forelimbs and blows the east wind

Is his shadow of yesterday?

Immortal —

2. 记忆中的荒原

摘掉荆冠
他从荒原踏来，
重新领有自己的运命。
眺望旷野里
气象哨
雪白的柱顶
横卧着一支安详的箭镞……

但是，
在那不朽的荒原 ——
不朽的
那在疏松的土丘之后竖起前肢
独对寂寞吹奏东风的旱獭
是他昨天的影子？
不朽的 ——

The wild goose breaks the cyclone under floating clouds at a high altitude

Shot by an arrow and lost in the dim light

The paragon of animals in a hot thorn bush

Stretching his neck and chasing lizards with stone tools

Is his shadow of yesterday?

In the immortal wasteland,

In the immortal dark night of the wasteland,

In the dark spiral staircase --

The restless haunting red fox,

The frightened, burrowed yellow weasel,

The unpredictable owls,

The wild cat,

The muntjac deer,

The phosphorescence,

... Are they his shadows of yesterday?

I do not understand oblivion.

When I look back at the mountain pass,

The setting sun is covered with colorful feathers,

— They are flower graves mourning the spring.

那在高空的游丝下面冲决气旋
带箭失落于昏溟的大雁、
那在闷热的刺棵丛里伸长脖颈
手持石器追食着蜥蜴的万物之灵
是他昨天的影子？
在不朽的荒原。
在荒原不朽的暗夜。
在暗夜浮动的旋梯 ——
那烦躁不安闪烁而过的红狐、
那惊犹未定倏忽隐遁的黄翔、
那来去无踪的鸥鸼、
那旷野猫、
那鹿麂、
那磷光、
……可是他昨天的影子？

我不理解遗忘。
当我回首山关，
夕阳里覆满五色翎毛，
—— 是一座座惜春的花冢。

3. The Other Shore

So, he heard.
The silent shore of Tibetans on the other side
The blades of the sutra wheels are running in great mercy.
He heard the broken raft rowing
the last cry.

When a storm sweeps everything
Sinking the lighthouse into the seabed,
Vortex and greed reach a tacit understanding,
The awake conscience of the other side
is the only shore of his life.

The dirty black clothes he took off here
left in the pier and let time wash,
His bleeding wounds all over the body
are naked in the light wind a lady blows.
The virgin covers her face with the back of her hand
Taking the purse from the robe, for him
Giving him protective herbs...

3. 彼岸

于是，他听到了。
听到土伯特人沉默的彼岸
大经轮在大慈大悲中转动叶片。
他听到破裂的木筏划出最后一声
长泣。

当横扫一切的暴风
将灯塔沉入海底，
旋涡与贪婪达成默契，
彼方醒着的这一片良知
是他唯一的生之涯岸。

他在这里脱去垢辱的黑衣
留在埠头让时光漂洗，
把遍体流血的伤口
裸陈于女性吹拂的轻风。
是那个以手背遮羞的处女
解下袍襟的荷包，为他
献出护身的香草……

In the wrestle between good and evil

The propagation and reproduction of love

Is older than death

And much braver!

Indeed,

When the old man goes to paradise

That's how he summons his beloved daughter and family

"Listen, you should live in harmony,

He is your family

Your brother,

My friend, and

My Son! "

在善恶的角力中
爱的繁衍与生殖
比死亡的戕残更古老、
更勇武百倍!
是的,
当那个老人临去天国之际
是这样召见了自己的爱女和家族
　"听吧,你们当和睦共处,
他是你们的亲人、
你们的兄弟,
是我的朋友,和
——儿子! "

4. The Gods

The reborn smile

is the bright moon after calamity.

I send the smiling moon

to conscientious people

in that era,

to tribes who have abandoned their surnames,

to the genus group that does not have graves.

to those who possess horses,

to those who fear fish and insects

to those who love wine bottles.

to those who around the campfire dance,

to those who breed grassland and create pastorals,

    The conqueror of beasts,

    the benefactor of birds,

    the connoisseur of cooking smoke,

    the free people favored by nature,

the idol I follow.

— Gods! Gods!

The gods should be you!

4. 众神

再生的微笑。
是劫余后的明月。
我把微笑的明月，
寄给那个年代
良知不灭的百姓。
寄给弃绝姓氏的部族。
寄给不留墓冢的属群。

那些占有马背的人，
那些敬畏鱼虫的人.
那些酷爱酒瓶的人。
那些围着篝火群舞的，
那些卵育了草原、耕作牧歌的，
　　猛兽的征服者，
　　飞禽的施主，
　　炊烟的鉴赏家，
　　大自然宠幸的自由民，
是我追随的偶像。

——众神！众神！
众神当是你们！

5. The Pet of Gods

This smile

is the proud mast of life that my ethereal khata sent

to the angle of

intersection of heaven and earth.

To the babysitter of soul.

to you —

    The little mother of the grassland.

At this moment,

Song of starlight

far from the sky

gives forth to me

frankincense as soft as children's skin;

Flowers at dawn

bloom for me in joy,

decoding the secret sign language of the soil.

You, standing on your bare toes

dry the milk dregs on the high platform.

Close to your shoulder,

baby's underwear hanging on a threadlet in front of the door

explain the eternal proverbs

with excitement as flags.

Cow dung pieces pasted on the wall

are your hand-made pictographic characters.

Gently picking off the charming words,

You turn around and give to your husband coming back,

ask him to store it in the hearth pit.

5. 众神的宠偶

这微笑
是我缥缈的哈达
寄给天地交合的夹角
生命傲然的船桅。
寄给灵魂的保姆。
寄给你 ——
　　　草原的小母亲。

此刻
星光之曲
又从寰宇
向我散发出
有如儿童肤体的乳香；
黎明的花枝
为我在欢快中张扬，
破译出那泥土绝密的哑语。

你哟，踮起赤裸的足尖
正把奶渣晾晒在高台。
靠近你肩头，
婴儿的内衣在门前的细丝
以旗帜的亢奋
解说万古的箴言。
墙壁贴满的牛粪饼块
是你手制的象形字模。
轻轻摘下这迷人的辞藻，
你回身交给归来的郎君，
托他送往灶坑去库藏。

(I see your flickering eyelashes

like the needle of millet with a smile;

I remember your frozen silence

is the arc light triggered by the electrode.)

That night, it was him

walking rashly towards you.

towards your chaste youth,

towards the cradle of your dreams,

towards the bitter fruit of your heart

with unalterable desire or lament,

He is more fearless than death --

He walks towards the other shore,

towards you

    the pet of gods!

（我看到你忽闪的睫毛
似同稷麦含笑之芒针；
我记得你冷凝的沉默
曾是电极触发之弧光。）

那个夜晚，正是他
向你贸然走去。
向着你贞洁的妙龄，
向着你梦求的摇篮，
向着你心甘的苦果……
带着不可更改的渴望或哀悼，
他比死亡更无畏 ——
他走向彼岸，
走向你
　　众神的宠偶！

6. The Encounter

He sits alone in the bare grassland.

Near his feet, the kiss of the sky fire left in the fragments of meteors

Behind his back, the river bed made up by nature —

spirits of fish, shells and seaweed

emerge from the Devonian period,

chase and play in the illusive water of daylight.

No graves,

Eagle's sky

interlaces rays of diamond edge.

Till then, he sees you come from a celestial mountain.

The four hoofs of the galloping horse suddenly stopped at the roadside.

Flowers swinging together for you

ring the bell of May.

— Aren't you happy, the princess of wilderness?

... But is there any village ahead?

He doesn't have to hide those dark stories

Those gilded scams, those... fairy tales,

He will tell you there is a crazy moment --

there is a severe winter in spring:

    Cool paper cap,

    Drunk rods and sticks,

    Bloodthirsty cats and dogs......

In this extremely cold world, nestlings

couldn't knock up in the dark

A door for shelter.

6. 邂逅

他独坐裸原。
脚边，流星的碎片尚留有天火的热吻
背后，大自然虚构的河床 ——
鱼贝和海藻的精灵
从泥盆纪脱颖而出，
追戏于这日光幻变之水。
没有墓冢，
鹰的天空
交织着钻石多棱的射线。

直到那时，他才看到你从仙山驰来。
奔马的四蹄陡然在路边站定。
花蕊一齐摆动，为你
摇响了五月的铃铎。
—— 不悦么，旷野的郡主？
……但前方是否有村落？
他无须隐讳那些阴暗的故事、
那些镀金的骗局、那些……童话，
他会告诉你有过那疯狂的一瞬 ——
有过那春季里的严冬：
        冷酷的纸帽，
        癫醉的棍棒，
        嗜血的猫狗……
天下奇寒，雏鸟
在暗夜里敲不醒一扇
庇身的门窦。

He will tell you: For the branch shining reappeared light,

the inevitable evil wind will blow away birds and sheep in the west

together...

While in the old cape where he was detained

Originally the altar of the mountain god,

In autumn, the call of swans can be heard now and then,

on the snowfield, there occasionally left with

the invitation from the white-lipped deer,

   — it used to be a good place...

   ...

   ...

Dusk is coming,

Quiet and soft.

Two dark grapes of a Tibetan girl ponder under starlight

Seem to tell him:

     — I understand.

     I offer.

     I believe...

The fluid glance at him from above

no longer fly the hesitant wings.

他会告诉你：为了光明再现的柯枝，
必然的妖风终将啼鸟和西天的羊群一同
裹挟……
而所在羁留的那个古老的山岬
原本是山神的祭坛，
秋气之中，间或可闻天鹅的呼唤，
雪原上偶尔留下
白唇鹿的请柬，
—— 那里原是一个好地方。……

…………
…………

黄昏来了，
宁静而柔和。
土伯特女儿墨黑的葡萄在星光下思索
似乎向他表示：
　　　—— 我懂。
　　　我献与。
　　　我笃行……

那从上方凝视他的两汪清波
不再飞起迟疑的鸟翼。

7. The Ship of Mercy

The magpies inside the garden
And the peacocks outside
— are the love songs of that place

At that, she blushes and smiles,
Calling the housedog back from guarding the flowered path,
Pulls the red silk scarf over her shoulder,
Hinting to the uninvited guest:

— And so,
I'll give you my saddle and bridle,
Shall I?
I'll give you my pony,
Shall I?
I'll give you my tent,
Shall I?
I'll give you my herb,
Shall I?

How beautiful —
Silver earrings irradiating the dusk,
The most ancient war trophies of human conscience!
Yes, in the struggle between good and evil,
The budding and flowering of love
is more ancient than the brutality of death
And a hundred times braver.

7. 慈航

花园里面的花喜鹊
花园外面的孔雀
—— 本土情歌于是，她赧然一笑，
从花径召回巡守的家犬，
将红绡拉过肩头，
向这不速之客暗示：

—— 那么，
把我的鞍辔送给你呢
好不好？
把我的马驹送给你呢
好不好？
把我的帐幕送给你呢
好不好？
把我的香草送给你呢
好不好？……

美呵，
黄昏里放射的银耳环，
人类良知的最古老的战利品！
是的，在善恶的角力中
爱的繁衍与生殖
比死亡的戕残更古老、
更勇武百倍！

8. Sukhavati (I)

The snow line......

The last extraordinary silver mountain,

becomes a crystal island in the blue sky,

belongs to the patrol of the lonely snow leopard.

But at the foot of the mountain, there is the green basin of earth,

insects flap their wings

weaving colorful winds.

The shepherd is gone, left with his tent,

left the stoves to the exhausted pasture.

The smoke of dung fire seems to be still summoning the vinous scent in

the fermenter,

as well the body heat under the animal skin mattress.

In the valley hard to discover,

the summer palace of herdsmen has been pitched,

The Tibetan baby with curly hair is like a kangaroo

protruding his head from his mother's robe,

surprised at the village just assembled.

8. 净土（之一）

雪线……
那最后的银峰超凡脱俗，
成为蓝天晶莹的岛屿，
归属寂寞的雪豹逡巡。
而在山麓，却是大地绿色的盆盂，
昆虫在那里扇动翅翼
梭织多彩的流风。
牧人走了，拆去帐幕，
将灶群寄存给疲惫了的牧场。
那粪火的青烟似乎还在召唤发酵罐中的
曲香，和兽皮褥垫下肤体的烘热。

在外人不易知晓的河谷，
已支起了牧人的夏宫，
土伯特人卷发的婴儿好似袋鼠
从母亲的袍襟探出头来，
诧异眼前刚刚组合的村落。

... a deer rushes toward the cliff,

twisting as half a soft gold circle,

instantly gone like the setting sun.

From afar came the cry of man,

the sound from deep down, long

hanging with the sound of hooves galloping in the mountain.

Happy people in mountains and valleys

protect their foreign visitors,

with an inherent broad mind

by no means yielding to imposed hardships

    As well as oppressive shame.

Here is the Sukhavati of conscience.

……一头花鹿冲向断崖，
扭作半个轻柔的金环，
瞬间随同落日消散。
而远方送来了男性的吆喝，
那吐自丹田的音韵，久久
随着疾去的蹄声在深山传递。
高山大谷里这些乐天的子民
护佑着那异方的来客，
以他们固有的旷达
决不屈就于那些强加的忧患
　　和令人气闷的荣辱。

这里是良知的净土。

9. Sukhavati (II)

... While behind the day
are bright stars.

It rises an adult's lullaby.
Muscles and bones have finished labor of the day,
no more sacred drunk dance is needed now.
Pestle and the agitation vat
Finally extinguished the ivory color

Along the river
silent fence —
ninety-nine yaks are precisely equidistant
walking slowly across the downy hills,
like a row of marching
fort.

The stove is still awake.
The bodies under fire light
Do not need to close shells in a dream.
These highly perfect works of art
as naked as their unbounded souls
bear the comfort of the night.

9. 净土（之二）

……而在白昼的背后
是灿烂的群星。

升起了成人的诱梦曲。
筋骨完成了劳动的日课，
此刻不再做神圣的醉舞。
杵杆，和奶油搅拌桶
最后也熄灭了象牙的华彩。

沿着河边
无声的栅栏 ——
九十九头牦牛以精确的等距
缓步横贯茸茸的山阜，
如同一列游走的
堆堡。

灶膛还醒着。
火光撩逗下的肉体
无须在梦中羞闭自己的贝壳。
这些高度完美的艺术品
正像他们无羁的灵魂一样裸露
承受着夜的抚慰。

— Life will last forever, and ever...

But in the dark green forest,

the tiger downhill is resting near the cliff,

it can no longer bear the painful loneliness,

flying over the thorny vine.

The parasitic flies

spark off the tiger's back,

in a hurry —

    seek for their another host...

——生之留恋将永恒、永恒……

但在墨绿的林莽，
下山虎栖止于断崖，
再也克制不了难熬的孤独，
飞身擦过刺藤。
寄生的群蝇
从虎背拖出了一道噼啪的火花，
急忙又 ——
        追寻它们的宿主……

10. The Ritual of Bathing

He is the "bride" to marry now!

On this gentle night
for the last request of the old man,
for the final intercourse of love,
he stood on the red carpet.
A shepherdess holds the censer
crouching at his feet,
gently blow at him the holy
smoke of cedar.
Everything is emotionless.
Everything is emotional.
Clairvoyant eyes
quietly gaze at
his subtle mind.

An upsurge of agitation.
Through the window, it sails slowly
thirty more, blessing New Year's Eve...
The candlestick looks further.
Oncoming —
He sees the Himalayan jungle
ignite a bright waterfall.
What is moving in the dim light
are thousands of towlines pulling the prayer wheel...

10. 沐礼

他是待娶的"新娘"了！

在这良宵
为了那个老人临终的嘱托，
为了爱的最后之媾合，
他屹立在红毡毯。
一个牧羊妇捧起熏沐的香炉
蹲伏在他的足边，
轻轻朝他吹去圣洁的
柏烟。
一切无情。
一切含情。
慧眼
正宁静地审度
他微妙的内心。

心旌摇荡。
窗隙里，徐徐飘过
三十多个祈福的除夕。……
烛台遥远了。
迎面而来——
他看到喜马拉雅丛林
燃起一团光明的瀑雨。
而在这虚照之中潜行
是万千条挽动经轮的纤绳……

He replies:

— "I understand.

    And I'm willing to."

The escorting messengers of wedding

hold him on the scarlet saddle,

along the way through the ice mountain, and

a torrential canyon.

Auspicious fire

light for him before sunrise.

At the stone gate, he gets off his horse

steps on the

goatskin specially prepared for him.

From the solid boat,

with an abhorrence of all prejudices

and an oath of beauty and goodness,

he resolutely leaped over the guard in front of the door

flames.

... Then

it comes to the golden drinking cup.

It's the burning water.

It is the butter lamp in the flower hall.

他回答：
——"我理解。
　　　我亦情愿。"

迎亲的使者
已将他搀上披红的征鞍，
一路穿越高山冰坂，和
激流的峡谷。
吉庆的火堆
也已为他在日出之前点燃。
在这处石砌的门楼他翻身下马
踏稳那一方
特为他投来的羊皮。
就从这坚实的舟楫，
怀着对一切偏见的憎恶
和对美与善的盟誓，
他毅然跃过了门前守护神狞厉的
火舌。

……然后
才是豪饮的金盏。
是燃烧的水。
是花堂的酥油灯。

11.The History of Love

…

…

In the immortal wasteland,

on the eve of dawn in the wilderness,

a cow in difficult labor

lying alone in frozen soil.

The frozen wind is cutting,

only a tramp is passing by here

sees the eyes for help

filled with painful tears.

Only he understands the specific symbol.

    — It's time:

    The one to be born must be born!

    The one to decay must quickly decay!

He read the date on the knot.

There is a pair of hands wearing jade bracelets

the fingertips digging into the thick walls simulated by night,

twisted braids

rub accumulated electric fire.

11. 爱的史书

············
············

在不朽的荒原。
在荒原那个黎明的前夕，
有一头难产的母牛
独卧在冻土。
冷风萧萧，
只有一个路经这里的流浪汉
看到那求助的双眼
饱含了两颗痛楚的泪珠。
只有他理解这泪珠特定的象征。
　　　　—— 是时候了：
　　　　该出生的一定要出生！
　　　　该速朽的必定得速朽！

他在绳结上读着这个日子。
那里，有一双佩戴玉镯的手臂
将指掌抠进黑夜模拟的厚壁，
绞紧的辫发
搓揉出蕴积的电火。

In the wilderness casting no light,

a baby was born.

The smiling tramp

he reads the day, carries on in the immortal

wasteland.

— You, a man in the desert, the smiling

Tramp, now that you are a derivative of various elements

Now that you are a polymer of elementary particles,

facing the maze of material with boundless changes,

you seem to have no need to worry,

also, no joy.

You may

once belonged to an

insect ovulating in prehistoric times;

you may belong to a drop of

floating fat melting in the ancient tableware of the gourmand

God

在那不见青灯的旷野，
一个婴儿降落了。

笑了的流浪汉
读着这个日子，潜行在不朽的
荒原。

　　　—— 你呵，大漠的居士，笑了的
　　　流浪汉，既然你是诸种元素的衍生物
　　　既然你是基本粒子的聚合体，
　　　面对物质变幻无涯的迷宫，
　　　你似乎不应忧患，
　　　也无须欣喜。

你或许
曾属于一只
卧在史前排卵的昆虫；
你或许曾属于一滴
熔落古鼎享神的
浮脂。

Imagine your oxidized previous life

It is weaved into the ribbon on the dress suit to hand down;

I hope your body in this life

will nurture a howling rose willow on a desert oasis.

You should be infinitely old, beyond time and space;

You should be infinitely young and possess an endless future.

You belong to the sum; hard to get

should not be reduced.

You are a logical choice of storm and thunder.

You should only reproduce the point where a particular space and time intersect.

But after all, you are a creature endowed with senses by this planet

the key is to intentionally conceive by time.

For the dark side of undisclosed genes,

to struggle ever hard for childbirth,

you are both the victim and owner,

you are also an ascetic monk and happy Buddha.

…

…

Indeed, in the wrestle between good and evil

the propagation and reproduction of love

is older than death

    and much braver!

设想你业已氧化的前生
织成了大礼服上传世的绶带；
期望你此生待朽的骨骸
可育作沙洲一株啸嗷的红柳。

你应无穷的古老，超然时空之上；
你应无穷的年轻，占有不尽的未来。
你属于这宏观整体中的既不可多得、
也不该减少的总和。

你是风雨雷电合乎逻辑的选择。
你只当再现在这特定时空相交的一点
但你毕竟是这星体赋予了感官的生物
是岁月有意孕成的琴键。

为了遗传基因尚未透露的丑恶，
为了生命耐力创纪录的拼搏，
你既是牺牲品，又是享有者，
你既是苦行僧，又是欢乐佛。

…………
…………

是的，在善恶的角力中
爱的繁衍与生殖
比死亡的戕残更古老、
    更勇武百倍！

12. The Elysium

When spring

ripens along with the incubator,

The grass and leaves peck through the shells of winter.

Is this accurate information delirium of fools!

All creatures contain endless mysteries:

Mountains rise from mantle movement;

halo of life is as beautiful as the corona;

combination of atoms forms galaxies in microcosm;

fragrant grass holds layers of color out of the soil.

Hedgehog is covered with sharp arrowheads...

When the avenues pass the procession of wreaths,

another team with only its name is in the shadow

marching forward.

    It's time.

    The one to resurrect has come back to life.

    The one to be born has already been born.

12. 极乐界

当春光
与孵卵器一同成熟，
草叶，也啄破了严冬的薄壳。
这准确的信息岂是愚人的谵妄！

万物本蕴涵着无尽的奥秘：
地幔由运动而矗起山岳；
生命的晕环敢与日冕媲美；
原子的组合在微观中自成星系；
芳草把层层色彩托出泥土。
刺猬披一身锐利的箭镞……

当大道为花圈的行列开放绿灯，
另有一支仅存姓名的队伍在影子里欢呼着
行进。
　　　是时候了。
　　　该复活的已复活。
　　　该出生的已出生。

But he --

takes off the crown of thorns

that comes from the wasteland

toward each of the tents.

He could not forget the snow mountain, the censer, and the peacock

plume.

He could not forget the numerous eyes on peacock plumes.

He already belongs to that sky.

He already belongs to that land.

He already belongs to that courtier without a court board.

But I,

with my orchid-shaped fingers

knock the echoes of the void again,

listen to the news of the loser about their defeat,

also unforgettable.

Yes, forever and ever --

The propagation and reproduction of love

is older than death

and much braver!

February 9, 1980 to June 25, 1981

而他 ——
摘掉荆冠
从荒原踏来,
走向每一面帐幕。
他忘不了那雪山,那香炉,那孔雀翎。
他忘不了那孔雀翎上众多的眼睛。
他已属于那一片天空。
他已属于那一片热土。
他已属于那一个没有王笏的侍臣。

而我,
展示状如兰花的五指
重又叩响虚空中的回声,
听一次失道者败北的消息,
也是同样地忘怀不了那一切。

是的,将永远、永远 ——
爱的繁衍与生殖
比死亡的戕残更古老、
　　更勇武百倍!

1980.2.9—1981.6.25

THE SUNRISE

I hear the sound of sunrise, rustling like the chirping of a cicada...

Rustling, rustling, rustling...

The subtle rustling sound,

    Quiet are the rivers, mountains and water urn beside the spring.

    It's the gourd ladle floating in the water urn.

But I can only hear the rustling sound.

Only hear the cock's oscillating comb.

Only hear the cone horn of the first waking blue sheep.

    In the narrow gap

    agronomists on donkeys set off together early.

But I can only hear the rustling red water

rustling and approaching from the eastern abyss.

March 29, 1982

日出

听见日出的声息蝉鸣般沙沙作响……
沙沙作响、沙沙作响、沙沙作响……
这微妙的声息沙沙作响。
　　静谧的是河流、山林和泉边的水瓮。
　　是水瓮里浮着的瓢。

但我只听得沙沙的声息。
只听得雄鸡振荡的肉冠。
只听得岩羊初醒的锥角。
　　垭豁口
　　有骑驴的农艺师结伴早行。

但我只听得沙沙的潮红
从东方的渊底沙沙地迫近

                    1982.3.29

ON THE ROAD: SUNSET IN SIGHT

Sunset in the desert:
It is farewell from the god of the sun.

In this wilderness, the fragrance of ammophila arenaria
lies his purple tassels.

Infinite generosity. He hands it over —
The monocycle of the sky only left half.

In the Asiatic desert
a camel has walked for nights.

March 17, 1983 draft

驿途：落日在望

大漠落日：
是日神之揖别。

这片原野，马兰草的幽香里
有他紫色的流苏。

无限慷慨。拱手相让，——
天涯的独轮车只剩半轮金环了。

亚细亚大漠
一峰连夜兼程的骆驼。

1983.3.17 初稿

THE PRAISE: IN THE NEW LANDSCAPE

Between the humps...
Between the humps and city
and apple orchard
and belt road
and furrow
and Neolithic sites... their tangent
boundary, the calling
modern iron tower forest
stands there.

Something is being destroyed.
Something is being created.

The totem disappeared.
The dead water revives. A generation of
clear fluid glance and standing
modern iron tower forests are together
calling.
Everything is irresistible.
Everything is regretless.
The smelting fire of Yangshao Culture
leaves the museum with
an unparalleled painted pottery basin. Time
suffuses the way of escorts
in the ancient and wild
dust.

赞美：在新的风景线

在驼峰……
在驼峰与城市
与苹果园
与环形路
与犁沟
与新石器时代遗址……相切的
边界，呼叫的
现代的铁塔林
矗立着。

有什么东西正被毁灭。
有什么东西正被创造。

图腾消亡了。
死水复活。一代
清澈的眼波和矗立的
现代的铁塔林一起
呼叫着。
一切无可抗拒。
一切无可反悔。
仰韶文化的炼火
给博物院留赠了一只
无双的彩陶盆。时间
把镖客的道路弥漫在
荒古的
尘埃。

While the hump reminds me that in the vast desert

the long howl of the wolf trembling all creatures

Just an inherent rhythm of nature.

Think about the evergreen scenery

Something is always being created.

Something is always being destroyed.

March 26 to April 8, 1983

而我从驼峰想到浩天大漠中
那曾使万物觳觫的一声狼的长嗥
原不过是大自然本身固有的律动。
想到在常新的风景线
永远有什么东西正被创造。
永远有什么东西正被毁灭。

                    1983.3.26—4.8

THE RANCHING GODDESS DORME

So, I will share your fragrance of snow on the iceberg steps.

I will read your poem hanging on the bull's horn year by year.

Hah, the incomparable beauty. You are invincible, you are successful --

You used to be clothed with sweet flowers for armor, banner,

and sword,

Man, horse, mountains, and honor of his hometown unite as one.

Songs and dances express good wishes for you.

The twining girls holding stone spinning wheels express good wishes for

you.

A grasshopper of the boy uses his long legs to pull up the cart of shepherd

kids.

Songs and dances express good wishes for you.

While I will follow your boat drifting in the green sea for a long,

and cast a gold anchor with the solemn pledge.

A third eye opens between your eyebrows: Youth

has got the musical rhythm under the beat of your unforgettable glance.

June to October, 1983

放牧的多罗姆女神

那么，我将分享你冰山台阶积雪的清芬。
我将逐年默诵你飘挂在牛角的诗教。

呵，无上之美。你无坚不克，无往不利 ——
你原是以娇嗔的繁花披作甲胄，披作旗帜，
披作剑锷，
人和马、和山岳、和故乡的荣名合而如一。
歌舞在为你而祝颂。
手持石纺轮的搓线女们在为你而祝颂。
少年的一匹高脚蚱蜢拉起牧童车。
歌舞在为你而祝颂。

而我将长远追随在你绿海上漂泊的帐幕，
以山之盟誓铸一黄金锚。

第三只眼睛在你眉间启开：青春
因你美目之顾眄而有了如歌的节奏。

1983.6—10

WE HAVE NO WAY BACK

A bold man plays with his sword under the moon,
singing "The swordsman has come back"...

It's an ancient bold man.
But we are not.
And we have no way back.

The place where we came from,
a wild land with a strong wind blowing yellow sand.
Only camels' dung leaves us
with blue kindling full of saltpeter smell
in the depth of winter's night, yes.
Yes, the naked dance of fire is indeed awfully beautiful and charming.
But we have no way back.

And we have no way but forward.
And we have no way back.

November 20, 1985

我们无可回归

狂人月下弹剑，
歌"长铗归来"……

是古狂人。
而我们不是。
而我们且无归去的路。

我们所自归来的那地方，
是黄沙罡风的野地。
仅有骆驼的粪便为我们一粒一粒
在隆冬之夜保存满含硝石气味的
蓝色火种。是的。
是的，那火焰之裸舞固然异常美妙魅人。
而我们无有归去的路。

而我们只可前行。
而我们无可回归。

1985.11.20

MIRACULOUS MIST

The new moon is setting. These are wild words apes are saying.

A breeze drifts away from time to time.

Quiet steps become my different inner self

Suddenly I'm frightened. At this time

The heavenly maiden on the cliff shows up

From stone fire, naked, bright, and graceful,

With long pretty hair.

She swings into the air, stretches her arms forward,

Jumps into the deep lake expecting to burn.

Firebirds swarm in an instant, cluttered and numerous

Thousands of hyaline bamboo shoot roots spray milk from the ground

The grand world is reborn bright.

My squinted pupils suddenly became black.

Open the cloak, I could hardly hear my ears,

For they have been integrated with the light already...

August 9, 1986

灵霄

新月傍落。山魈的野语。
细风时时飘忽掠去。
悄行的步履成为异我之存在
猛可地惊怵。这时
悬崖上的天女
已从石火裸现，鲜艳，窈窕，
长披美发丝。
她转体腾空，前展双臂，
一头跃向期待燃烧的深湖。
瞬刻火鸟群飞，林林总总
一千条透明的笋根从地底喷射琼液
盛大世界升起再生之光华。
我眯闭的瞳孔骤然洞黑。
掀开斗篷，听到自己的耳朵不复存在，
早与光明合为一体……

1986.8.9

THE COOL-TONE SCENERY WITH A SMALL HOTEL IN IT

The rainy season is prolonged. Thunder and lightning retreat overnight, and new wheat
Germinates early at the ear of wheat. Gravity bends
Slowly on the knee. My departure is delayed repeatedly,
Time adds another growth ring.

A foggy morning. The bead curtain of the small hotel waves red and green in the eastern desert
The joyful melody of the drum band goes along with the camel team.
A bullock cart parks at the door, absent with the carter there
The bull under the yoke is generously and unworldly chewing grass in the basket.
The little sheep tied at the rear of the cart looks back at the scenery
With a slight move, it feels the upcoming destination and cries lonely.

The grasshopper cage is hung on the window lattice,
The noisy sun and moon runs in an arc hand in hand,
The rich mountain forest,
It has gained a few pounds more than last year.

In the broken bridge and forked road,
the stone pillar top holds a dewdrop that has witnessed thousands of years,
vaguely like the eyes of a vegetable.
I could just spit out one word: —— Hai!

August 15, 1986

冷色调的有小酒店的风景

雨季延长。雷电一夕苟且，新麦
于穗头提前萌发。重力在膝盖
缓缓弯曲。我的行期再三耽搁，
岁月又添加一圈年轮。

雾晨。小酒店珠帘红绿微动，东方沙漠
鼓乐喜庆的旋律自店家结队驼行。
门首一辆牛车，车主不在，轭下老牛
闷头嚼食筐中草料慷慷慨慨与世无争。
车尾拴系的绵羊回顾小酒店珠帘红绿
微动，意识到即将的归宿而啼叫孤独。

蝈蝈笼悬在窗桹，
日月的喧哗弧面转接，
山林的浓郁，
比去年多了几斤分量。

断桥歧路，柱头石核嗑一颗露珠瞪视已越千年，
茫然似植物人的眼神。
我仅吐出一个字：—— Hai ！

1986.8.15

FIRE SACRIFICE

Tall trees draw on big winds, and silent seas raise huge waves.

— Cao Zhi: "The Yellow Sparrows in Wild Field"

1. The Empty Sorrow

There will be no more secrets.

The night has lost its meaning of curtains,

Trauma will not add more sense of security at night.

The sound of waves is crueler than in the day.

Man-faced birds fly to the river bank before dawn, guiding the way to sing.

Is it for atonement? Is it for suffering? Or prayer to gods?

The night has lost its meaning of repair, harder than crystal and ice.

The world is no need to hide; we understand each other thoroughly at a glance.

Idols fall down in rows but deliver empty sorrow

To the warriors carrying a halberd,

Warrior, warrior, warrior

They tread down the rusty shadows,

The broken glass has rattled in the fading blue from the inclined plane.

燔祭

　　高树多悲风，海水扬其波。
　　　　—— 曹植：《野田黄雀行》

1. 空位的悲哀

不将有隐秘。
夜已失去幕的含蕴，
创伤在夜色不会再多一分安全感。
涛声反比白昼更为残酷地搓洗休憩的灵魂。
人面鸟又赶在黎明前飞临河岸引领吟唤。
是赎罪？是受难？还是祈祷吾神？
夜已失去修补含蕴，比冰霜还生硬。
世界无需掩饰，我们相互一眼看透彼此。
偶像成排倒下，而以空位的悲哀
投予荷戟的壮士，
壮士壮士壮士
踩牢自己锈迹斑斑的影子，
碎玻璃已自斜面哗响在速逝的幽蓝。

2. The Solitary Indignation

Against the heaven wall
Solo dancer beats
the target hole
Flying like snowflakes
It's the solitary indignation.

In beautiful sorrow
As thick as ice-capped Osaka
like a laser harp
I tap with my slender fingers
Shining like a red candle.

Eyes closed. Dregs floated.
The hustle sound of Blue Army's clapper.
The mutilated limbs of runaway soldiers stooping over.
The previewed death
March, along with the mountains and forests in my childhood,
Already left cruel seeds for young adults.

Nature is moaning.
Cutting wind sweeps from behind.

2. 孤愤

天堂墙壁
独舞者拳击
靶孔
如雪片飞扬
孤愤。

美丽忧思
厚如冰山大坂
如一架激光竖琴
叩我以手指之修长
射如红烛。

闭目。沉滓泛起。
蓝军紧促的梆子声。
士兵弯身奔逃的残肢。
预习的死亡
与我儿时的山林同步逼进，
早为少年留下残酷种芽。

大自然悲鸣。
冰风自背后袭来。

3. Temple of Light

Here it is too bright. Chill pours like a silver lake.

The frozen ice on the cliff is like molten tin hanging on the candlestick.

Here it is too bright. The space of gyration was once a burning sea of prominence.

How can I climb a cliff full of beaks?

How can I take a winter swimming in the hanging river?

How can I bear the limpid jade palace?

It's too pure. There is no curl of the smoke.

The wings and tail of the vulture on the dome do not move,

of no possibility of being swallowed in my look.

Here it is too bright.

I have seen my different inner self go beyond thousands of years,

The veins are clear in red and blue, like carved crystal bodies in the nude

Bearing the eternal drying sun.

3. 光明殿

这里太光明，寒意倾泻如银湖。
峭壁冻冰如烛台凝挂的熔锡。
这里太光明，回旋的空间曾是日珥燃烧的火海。
我如何攀登生满鸟喙的绝壁？
我如何投入悬挂的河流作一次冬泳？
我如何承受澄明的玉宇？
太纯洁了。烟丝不见袅袅。
穹顶兀鹰翼尾不动，不可被目光吞噬。
这里太光明。
我看到异我坐化千年之外，
筋脉纷披红蓝清晰晶莹透剔如一玻璃人体
承受着永恒的晾晒。

4. The Structure of Shock

The structure of shock brings a shocking gem to emotion.

Light frees night. Sky penetrates the lake.

Lovers' cheek dance suddenly blows the chilly wind.

The cave of earth ignites the remaining grease of life.

The big road gets throes every day.

The men and women lay down every day.

The waxy human brain cracks like pomegranate petals every day.

The fire sacrifice line of growth ring every day.

Every moment is the last.

Every moment becomes a used fortress.

Quiet, quiet as you are always

It is a cry of "such a good child".

4. 噩的结构

噩的结构为情感带来惊愕的宝石。
灯光释放黑夜。天空穿透湖水。
情人的贴面舞骤然冷风嘶嘶。
地穴燃起生命残剩的油脂。

每天的阵痛的大路。
每天的放倒的男子女子。
每天蜡质般绽开的人脑如石榴碎瓣。
每天的时轮的燔祭线。
每一刹那都是最后时刻。
每一刹那都成故垒。

宁馨儿，你如此的宁馨儿
原是一声"这么好的孩儿"。

I am so lonely and longing for a nymph:

Her glossy black hair flutters for me at the edge of the basin,

Like the flapping curtain in the country tavern.

Scattered bugles have tilted due to the blowing and minting of the desert.

Hematite ore powder covers trees overnight,

Raising the flag of roses.

Dazzling male material stabs like twigs of the chaste tree.

In the land of culture and ethics,

The solitary journey of a Taoist turns into a far cry away from the truth.

In the skull ground of ancestral remains

A busybody would be lucky enough to take a skeleton of a woman,

It satisfies the peeping desire stretching thousands of years.

Lying flat on the marble mourning bed and listening to the vocal songs,

Quietly to feel the beauty of shock lasting forever.

我如此孤独而渴望山鬼了：
盆地边缘她以油黑的薄发为我而翩翩飘曳，
如乡村酒垆飞动的酒帘。
零落的号筶已因沙漠鼓铸而倾斜。
赤铁矿粉末一夜之间挂满千棵树，
而举起了玫瑰之旗。
耀目的男性物质如荆条扎手。
衣冠文物之邦，
道学士的孤旅南辕北辙。
在祖先遗体熟化的骷髅地
好事之徒每若得幸会抱还一架女人骨殖，
而满足了跨越千年的窥视欲。

平卧大理石灵床听人声伴唱，
默默感受罹的美艳百代永垂。

5. Capital Qianmen · The Lion-faced Man

In Capital Qianmen

The Mongolian barbecue from American California against the mosaic curtain wall of the restaurant raises dreamy smoke. So the parking lot is covered in the dusk of pasture.

The cowboy returns late.

Every drop of sunset crackles like hissing hot oil.

Every dust particle shines like a splendid golden button.

I walk towards the lion-faced man squatting by the ring river.

I lean against the jade foundation pillar and feel the dreamy night increase bit by bit.

I secretly glimpse the quiet lion-faced man as a boy glimpses his father.

I take a secret glimpse at the fierce silence of the lion-faced man.

I think his forearm tendon has a slight twitch.

I think his forearms bathing in water just pull back from the plow stick for reclamation.

I think his slight frown hides deep gloom.

I think his forehead shows some jeer of profound significance.

I think his ringed curly hair looks graceful and elegant.

I think his fiery pupils seem weary.

I know well such potential depression is depression I rarely understand.

I know well such depression is the deep reason why I am so shocked.

The pain of a lion-faced man is the pain we directly inherited.

5. 京都前门·狮面人

京都前门
餐馆马赛克幕墙美国加州蒙古烤肉的烟燧如梦升起。停车坪遂罩
在牧场的黄昏。
牛仔归迟。
每一滴落日浑如嘶声炸裂的热油脂。
每一粒尘嚣亮如时装辉煌的金拷钮。

我走向环城河边蹲坐的狮面人。
我依傍玉石础柱感觉梦幻的夜色逐刻加重。
我偷觑沉默的狮面人如同孩子偷觑父亲。
我偷觑狮面人威猛的沉默。
我感觉他前臂肌腱略一抽动。
我感觉他浴在水边的前臂才挽罢垦荒的犁杖。
我感觉他眉间微蹙的悒郁造境遥深。
我感觉他瓣额几许嘲讽悠然意远。
我感觉他如环散开的鬣毛雍容儒雅。
我感觉他如火照人的瞳孔透出疲惫。
我深知如此潜在的悒郁是我难得洞悉的悒郁。
我深知如此的悒郁是使我如此震撼的深刻原因。
狮面人的痛楚是我们直接嫡承的痛楚。

6. Xiao

Hypocrisy makes people weary.

Love has been materialized, while gold does not buy everything.

The sense of loss is an inborn melancholy.

Life is like a trapped fly in captivity,

It is always hopeless to find the way out, and there is always an endless

mystery.

What to do with reason and intellect?

Image is deconstructed, language does not make sense.

Is it difficult to die?

Just a whimper and tears pour down,

The wriggling mouth suddenly became the prison of last words.

6. 箫

伪善令人怠倦。
情已物化，黄金也不给人逍遥。
失落感是与生俱来的惆怅。
人世是困蝇面对囚镜，
总是无望的夺路，总有无底的谜。
理智何能？图象尸解，语言溃不成军。
死有何难？只需一声呜咽便泪下如雨，
蠕动的口型顿时成为遗言的牢狱。

Everything is sown with the same hands at the same time.

Everything is made in the same ancient vine by the same root.

The snake of destiny has already displayed a terrible warning color on the altar.

Sparks are chasing in the hiss of fuse from time to time.

Fear is a human nature.

But misery is weak in nature, and Taoism breeds suspicions.

No more questions about odiousness exemption.

Being aware of the Demon King is to understand God.

Either curse or praise.

Either for moaning or shouting.

Lack of confident, flattering would make up.

With no intention to raise a hubbub, please keep quiet.

God is missing, the bell rings back to bronze times,

Stream leads to spring hole,

Dusk goes up to dawn,

The physical property is renewed original.

Witches, witches, my eyes are the bathtub for your dirty games.

Listen to the quiet Xiao.

November 30, 1988

一切是在同一时辰被同一双手播种。
一切是在同一古藤由同一盘根结实。
命运之蛇早在祭坛显示恐怖的警告色。
火花时时在导火索的嘶鸣中追步。
恐惧原是人类的本性。
而痛苦生性孱弱，道学孳乳多疑。
别再提问丑恶可免否。
理解了魔王也就理解了上帝。
不是诅咒就是赞美。不为呻吟就为呐喊。
自信不足则谄笑有加。无心鼓噪则请沉默。
神已失踪，钟声回到青铜，
流水导向泉眼，
黄昏上溯黎明，
物性重展原初。
巫女巫女，我的眼波是你们狎戏的浴盆。
听淡淡的箫。

1988.11.30

FAR AWAY FROM THE CITY

Far away from the city, carter's carriage stumbled along the torrential river.

Water smoothes a horse's belly; someone worries cold water hurts the horse's bone.

The northern fields are vast and boundless, lonely horse legs

Move orderly in horse bells with a comfortable gait.

The sad eyes fall into a sad river and grow out from the horizon

Curled hyena hair.

December 30, 1989

远离都市

远离都市，车夫的马车在流渐的河道颠踬驱驶。
水流抹平马腹，有人惦记水寒伤马骨。
北方的原野广袤无垠，伶仃的马肢
在马铃散落中措动节肢，步态安适。
忧戚的眼神掉在忧戚的河道，天边长出
蜷曲的鬣毛。

1989.12.30

HER

I wake up, recalling futile memories. In search of the memory cabin, I could not find any of her traces in my life. I clearly remembered she was my only best friend in my dream now (no, not just my best friend). Now that I have been expelled from the door of dreams, my memory of her has also been stripped completely, even lost her looks: She was just an idea mixed with dreams. Now, I am on the back of the dream.

How wonderful: Life, in fact, has two kinds of itself, but it is difficult for me to say which is more pleasant or true. But, certainly, Lethe exists everywhere, like a waterfall. It not only filters me from my body surface but also penetrates into every aspect of my spiritual flesh. I will, at last, just leave a piece of diluted shadow and finally eliminate it in nihility. But now I am sure that I remember that person. I am confident that I still have the inexplicable warmth given by that person in my heart. Whether this fact is happiness or cruelty! This situation reminds me of a group of prisoners of death who whispered to each other in the ear a moment before their execution 40 years ago. Then I could only think from a child's perspective and thought: What is the point of their talk?

September 10, 1990

她

梦醒，我作着徒劳无益的回忆，搜尽记忆之舱也丝毫寻找不到她在我生活中的影踪，而刚才在梦中还分明记得她是我唯一的挚友（不，还不仅仅是挚友）。现在我被逐出了梦之门，有关她的记忆也随即被剥夺得一干二净，甚至于丢失了她的容貌：她只是一个与梦浑融的念头。现在，我是在梦的背面了。

多奇妙：人生实际上有着两种自我，然而哪个更惬意或更真实我都难于启齿。但可肯定忘川是无处不有的存在，悬如瀑布，不仅要从我体表，且渗透到灵肉的每一切面将我过滤似的淘洗尽净，最终的我也只将剩下一片冲淡的虚影而最终消弭于虚无。但我现在还确信记得那个她人，自信在我心间还保留着那个她人给予的一团莫名的温热，这事实究竟是幸福还是残忍！这种情形让我记起四十年前看到的一群死刑犯在处决前片刻的接耳交谈，那时，我仅能从一个孩子的眼光思考，心想：他们的交谈究竟还有什么意义？

1990.9.10

CROSS OVER THE RIVER
— DO NOT CROSS

Cross over the river. Listen to the struggling diastrophism of time sequence on the riverbed:

The watery wind, white fog and coolness are brought gently here.

Oh, drifting, drifting, drifting forever

A spirit of holiness in front as real as it is, the flatterers already feel it vast and mighty.

Now I can cast off my flesh and run away,

Throw as food for the dancing eagles in the middle of the great expanse.

If the essence of personality is only the burning will,

I happen to expect you to give that spark.

Love is the source and also the destination.

The river barge is sailing northward against the current,

Let me see it as an unchanging sacrifice of a life contract.

As the wave marks in the riverbank like a skull cut from a mountain,

The brick building is still a great undertaking for thousands of years.

They are old. When a couple stands in a huge crowd of people as obsessed as a tree.

June 10, 1991

涉江
——别S

涉江。听时序在河床艰难错动：
水风、白雾与凉意徐徐推来。
啊，漂流，漂流，永在地漂流……
前有灵犀圣洁如现，已令阿谀者感到大气沛然。
此际我可脱卸肉体如弃敝屣，
为森茫之中盘舞的鹰群抛食。
如果人格的精义只在燃烧的意志，
我恰已期待你给予那一粒星火。
爱是源泉也会是归宿。
大江拖驳正领航逆流北进，
让我看作人生契约无改之祭仪。
想那江岸巨石切痕凿凿如自山岳割取的脑颅，
被砌造的关楼犹然万年大业。
都已苍老。当一对情侣站立人海执迷如树。

1991.6.10

THE REMAINING DRAFT IN 1991

I restart my journey. I was born a lively person but depressed in nature. I used to work in the vast unknown wilderness. The sudden impulse in my chest would make me stop farming and quickly engrave the meaning of some enlightenment in the plowstick. I was once a child under the stove of the subtropical sun, admiring gods with my mother through the protection of the temple. I advocate the spirit of reality; I let the light of reason shine through my cornea. Still, I do not always reject the transcendental perception of the other world in the empirical world. The paradoxical existence of reality always has modernity for me. I understand why the calligrapher Zhang Xu walks wildly shouting when drunk after writing. I also understand why the calligrapher Huai Su is intoxicated with wine and splashes ink on doors, walls, vessels and clothes within his sight. Therefore, we see a changeable sky with thunder and lightning after he writes. They have mighty hearts. Yes, I should deeply understand why the Chu poet chanted "Tian Wen" to present one hundred and more questions to heaven. I will start my journey again. My new journey is still the home search. Every day at dawn for a long time, the same bird flew to the river and called to a quiet bird in the dark with its sweet cry. I regard it as a call to me. But I am not quiet. The soul's desire can only be compared to the feeling of a drowning person. I know the home in search of, even if as small as a nest, but it belongs to me.

June 28, 1991

1991 年残稿

重新开始我的旅行。我天性是一个活泼的人，但又本质抑郁。我曾在不为人知的广漠原野耕耘，胸中突然的冲动会让我辍耕，而将某种启示的含义速刻在犁杖。我曾是亚热带阳光火炉下的一个孩子，在庙宇的荫庇底里同母亲一起仰慕神祗。我崇尚现实精神，我让理性的光芒照彻我的角膜，但我在经验世界中并不一概排拒彼岸世界的超验感知。悖论式的生存实际，于我永远具有现代性。我理解书法家张旭何以乘醉举笔呼喊狂走。我也理解书法家怀素酒酣兴发为何将所目遇之门墙器皿衣物尽数挥毫泼墨无一幸免，因之龙蛇夭矫、雷鸣电掣。心有浩然之气啊。是的，我应当深解咏作《天问》的楚国诗人何必一气向苍天发出一百几十种诘难了。重新开始我的旅行吧。我重新开始的旅行仍当是家园的寻找。很久以来，每天破晓，总有同一只鸟儿飞来河边，以悦耳的啼鸣向着幽冥中一只沉默的鸟儿呼唤，我当作是对我的呼唤。但我并不沉默。灵魂的渴求只有溺水者的感受可为比拟。我知道我寻找着的那个家园即便小如雀巢，那也是我的雀巢。

1991.6.28

THE TWILIGHT OF IDOLS

In the distant Hindu Kush Mountains

The religious leader Zarathustra goes back to the west, falls down in the

crags and spits blood,

The vaporific blood burns on the ancient ice peak

Like the tulips sought by Persian court poets in their dreams.

He feels the life in the dying moment again reflect the dawn color.

But the blood is nearly dried up, and it is suddenly dark.

The heroes back to the west fell into the eastern sea far away

His favorite firebird still rose as usual.

Everything is in expectation: So the power of love destroys the

demonized hardships.

August 3, 1991

偶像的黄昏

遥远的兴都库什山里
西还的教主查拉图斯特拉累倒在巉岩大口吐血，
蒸发之血气在亘古的冰峰燃烧
好像波斯宫廷诗人热梦中寻求的郁金香。
他感觉弥留时刻的生命重又透射出那一黎明色。
但是血近枯竭，转瞬天黑。
西还的壮士感觉在遥远的东方海面
他所心仪的火鸟仍如常日冉冉升起。
一切都在意中：魔难于是也因爱力的完全消解而同归灭寂。

1991.8.3

THE GUEST FROM AUTUMN

The fierce wind cuts the ears of a horse

It's autumn again when the coachman hears the wind

The vast field still walks troika

Broad loneliness spreads in every sound of autumn

Nihility is like its beginning

One layer of yellow sand falls

Two layers of yellow sand fall

Three layers of yellow sand fall

The coachman always holds his generosity

The sorrow of autumn only left to the autumn guests before the wind.

August 27, 1991

秋客

厉风刺马耳
马车夫听风又是秋了
茫茫原野还是行走着三套马车
博大的寂寞在每一声秋里扩散
虚无正如初始
一层黄沙落
两层黄沙落
三层黄沙落
慷慨总还是马车夫的慷慨
对秋扼腕只余风前的秋客

1991.8.27

THE FACIAL MAKEUP

For the pain of tolerance, the hypostatic person

Has cooled down his smile and cleared away to a desolation.

The trickle of emotion immediately confines the ice for a deep reason.

Therefore, the most hypostatic mask becomes a bastion of iron guarded

by the righteous people to live and die with it:

So many war horses. So many abandoned corpses.

Go ahead; I have already been depressed.

June 30, 1992

面谱

为那隐忍之痛，本质的人
已将笑容坚壁清野留下一片荒冷。
为了那深深的原因，情感的涓流顷刻封冰。
于是最具本质的面谱遂成为与之共存亡的义士据守其间的铜墙铁壁：
许多具战马。许多具弃尸。

去吧，吾已颓丧。

1992.6.30

THE SUFFERING FLOWER
— THOUGHTS OF THE IIVING ABOUT LIVING

The road bends, and the backward buildings move backward more
quickly

Listen to the ticking clock sending out a constant alarm.

There are inelastic springs in the sky. Good. Time is rioting.

We have been thinking about escaping for a long time. But we will not
get old faster.

The autumn wind blew as we crossed the road.

I feel my girlfriend is stung by her own vision.

Suddenly her face changed. She turns around, jumps away, and runs a
few steps,

Stooping to rescue a red flower from under the speeding wheel.

A suffering red flower in the war against time.

Hold my gift, please. --My girlfriend said.

She raises her little fingertip, combs the petals and hands the flower to
me.

花朵受难
——生者对生存的思考

大路弯头，退却的大厦退去已愈加迅疾
听到滴答的时钟从那里发出不断的警报。
天空有崩卷的弹簧。很好，时间在暴动。
我们早想着逃离了。但我们不会衰老得更快。

我们横越马路时刮起秋风。
感觉女伴被自己的视觉蜇痛了。
她突然变色，侧转身跳开去，猛跑几步，
俯身从飞驰而过的车轮底下抢救起一枝红花朵。
时间对抗中一枝受难的红花朵。
快抱好我的献与。—— 女伴说。
她翘起小指尖梳理一下鳞瓣花页这样递给我。

This is the first flower I have received as a gift.

Xiuhuang, you know how this dahlia is as frightened as a bird on a wire

Falling in the driveway? It looks like I have nowhere to live.

Do you have any idea whether the suffering dahlia is drunk or awake?

It looks like I have nowhere to live.

My girlfriend and I stand by the road with dahlias.

No ambulance stopped, and no one heard dahlia calling.

But I feel the flower is turning black and purple... Is it drunk or awake?

I speak to myself: It should be awake if it is not drunk.

The white mansion looks bright under the setting sun and recedes the light further and further.

Time collapses and withers as the earth. Xiuhuang, let's get away quickly.

October 10, 1992

这是我生平接受馈赠的第一枝花朵了。
修篁啊，你知道大丽花是怎样如同惊弓之鸟
坠落在车道的么？似我无处安身。
你知道受难的大丽花是醉了还是醒着？
似我无处安身。
女伴与我偕同大丽花伫立路畔。
没有一辆救护车停下，没有谁听见大丽花呼叫。
但我感觉花朵正变得黑紫……是醉了还是醒着？
我心里说：如果没醉就该是醒着。

夕阳底下白色大厦回光返照，退去更其遥远。
时间崩溃随地枯萎。修篁，让我们快快走。

1992.10.10

THE SPIRAL HAIR BUN

On the other side of the spiral hair bun, a chorus of virgins begins at the
right moment:
... Alleluia, Alleluia, Alleluia...
The cadence of Alleluia resounded through the air.
I firstly just want to have a rest, then I feel refreshed and spirited,
The lonely travelers far from home seem surprised to hear the horn in the
mountains.
But I have no intention of hunting dogs' race.
My journey is a long sword drawn into the scabbard.
Now I want to return. Look, the dust has settled, and the great tranquility
brings propitiousness,
Among the Dharma doctrine, the deer chirps open gem blue light.
It looks like over there, they are wearing gold Buyao on the head and
jade Ruyi on the waist,
Pretty girls, a great many show me their black spiral hair bun,
It is a fantasyland as in a dream. There is no road beyond the continent. A
black vortex spurts out a stream of life.
Alleluia, Alleluia, what an emotional call?
It made all the people stooping for gold coins look back together.
So I hear the choir of virgins continue to sing another song,
It's like an angel preaching the gospel.
And I'm still sorry! Frustration? Depression? Indignation? Desolation?...

螺髻

螺髻那面，贞童的合唱应时开始：
……阿里露亚、阿里露亚、阿里露亚……
抑扬顿挫的阿里露亚响彻远近空蒙。
我先只渴望休憩，继而神清气爽思维振奋，
好像天涯孤旅蓦然听到山中号角。
但我终无意猎犬的角逐。
我的征途是入鞘近半之长剑。
且萌念归去。看啊，尘埃落定，大静呈祥，
法林珠苑，鹿鸣呦呦绽开宝蓝光。
好像那壁厢，头戴金步摇，身佩玉如意，
有女如云，示我云鬓乌螺髻，
烟梦迷茫。路断海州。黑色涡旋喷射生命流。
阿里露亚阿里露亚，那是何等动心的呼叫？
竟令弯身大道寻拾金币的众生一起回首。
于是我听见贞女的合唱曲随之续作一片，
好像天使布道谆谆播撒福音。
尚还抱憾！失意？沮丧？饮恨？凄楚？……

I feel the boundary between myself and the material becomes blurry. I am assimilated by things and gradually free and unfettered.

But I still feel tired. A man's tiresome is tiresome most worthy.

Chondrosis has long been an incurable human disease.

Do they still try to tighten your spine and play the clang rhythm of the saw zither?

Too many humiliations. Up a gum tree. Only great wisdom speaks little.

But your remarkable spiral hair bun shows me the thermonuclear reaction.

I remember experiencing shifts dramatically, like the garden in different seasons,

Out of pain, I couldn't feel the sharp blade but the breeze on my face.

Alleluia, Alleluia, a camel team, is knocking the west with their pass and crossing the desert.

Such a bun is the home of my sense of beauty.

December 6, 1992

我竟已感觉自己边缘模糊与物同化渐入逍遥。
还是倦怠啊。男子汉的倦怠最足倦怠了。
软骨病早已成人类之宿疾不可救药。
还试图绷紧脊椎奏出锯琴铮铮的旋律？
屈辱诸多。进退维谷。唯大智无言。
但你卓砾不凡的螺髻为我显示热核之反应。
我记起着经验如同四季花园剧烈转换，
失去疼痛，不觉利刃阉割竟如清风徐徐吹我。
阿里露亚阿里露亚正有驼队持牒叩关西渡流沙。
如许螺髻却是我美感的归宿。

1992.12.6

I SEE A HOLLOW MAN SCUFFLE IN THE STORM

The storm comes over the border.

I look out from the corner of the building where I live, seeing the dense raindrops approaching quickly, dark clouds rolling and billowing, and shining gold rings scattered among them, like the edge of a gold shield. I have a sense of security in the barrack camp. I appreciate it.

What do I see? Albatrosses soar across the ocean? Free petrels and eagles?... It is just a few pieces of old newspaper flying up from the streets and a colored plastic bag chasing after them until they are too high to disappear. What else do I see? Why is it so horrible? A white dress hanging on the skyscraper. Oh, the hanging woman lonely flies with the hook and does handsprings. No one is going to rescue her. The hollow woman swishes and exhales cold air. The hollow woman is puffed up by the storm and shivers, then she suddenly is held upside down, hollow inside; what a human pelt. But even human pelt always has a moment of anger. Even the hollow cannot bear being trampled. No one comes to rescue her. I see it raise its arms and quickly slide along the wire to the other end. It has firmly held the iron pestle supporting the wall and would like to uproot it. It would rather be torn apart than humiliated completely. I heard the wall shaking. I heard the storm getting fiercer. I pray that this painful scene will end soon, even if that hollow one tears itself into pieces and floats from here, away, away...

May 22, 1993

我见一空心人在风暴中扭打

暴风雨压境而来。

我从栖身的楼隅朝外窥望，见雨脚快步逼进，乌黑的云头翻腾滚动，有耀目的金环饰错落其间，如金盾的沿口。我领有一种营垒中人的安全感。我欣赏着。

我看到了什么？信天翁越洋高翔？自由的海燕、雄鹰？……是街巷飞扬而起的三五张废旧报纸，连同一只彩塑包装袋正扶摇直上，竞相角逐，愈逐愈高终至不见。我还看到了什么？为何这般骇人？——一袭白色连衣裙，悬空吊晾在摩天楼台。啊，这女吊，孤零零，正随吊钩飞旋，翻着斤斗，没有谁去搭救。这空心人嗖嗖有声，吐着冷气。这空心人被风暴吹得鼓鼓囊囊，瑟瑟发抖，而转瞬间又被倒提着抽打一空活脱脱一张人皮。但即便人皮也总有愤怒的一瞬。即便空心也不堪蹂躏。没有谁去搭救。我见它举起双臂沿着铁丝快速滑向一端，果真扑打而去。它已牢牢抱紧支撑在墙面的铁杆恨不得连根拔却。它宁可被撕裂四散，也不要完整地受辱。我听到墙体在摇动。我听到风暴更激烈。我在心里祈祝这痛苦的一幕快快结束，哪怕让空心人撕作碎片从此飘去、飘去……

1993.5.22

KEEP AWAY FROM POETS

A lady who was warned to "keep away from poets" asked me: "Are poets really melancholy daydreaming, so they are untouchable?" I looked at her, speechless for a moment. Wrathful for those pure technical experts who instilled such a superficial understanding of materialism in her. In the cold eyes of these people, emotion is a dangerous virus, while they are the strong support of women worldwide.

I am speechless. Looking at her white body being covered by a layer of haze, I have no chance to protect it: The pursuit of spirit cannot be replaced and interpreted by greed. Some moistened slander is taking effect. I could feel the piercing cold.

But I gloated and said to her: "Yes, madam, please do what you are told!"

October 20, 1993

勿与诗人接触

一位受到警告"勿与诗人接触"的女士问我:"诗人果真是做着白日梦的忧郁的人,故而不可接触吗?"我望着她,一时无语。为着在她周围向她灌输了这种物质主义浅薄认识的纯技术专家们激愤不已。在这些人冰凉的眼里,情感是危险的病毒,而他们自己才是普天下女人们强大的靠背。

我无语。望着她洁白的身体正为一层阴霾蒙蔽,我却无缘保护:精神的追求不能被贪欲替代、释解。一种浸润之潜正在发生作用。我觉出刺骨的寒凉。

但我却幸灾乐祸了,肯定地对她说:"没错,夫人,就请这么办!"

1993.10.20

THE TEMPLE

Temple is nothing about building. Nothing about offices. Beyond materials.

Even nothing to do with the practice of celibacy. Nor involved in the wake. Even beyond languages.

The temple is held by a plump plain hand under the bright sky on the other side of the world.

It is beyond movement and quietude and has nothing to do with contributions or benefits.

I gaze and feel a primitive meaning with my whole body and mind.

I would barely call this state of life "solemness".

January 25, 1994

寺

寺，非关建筑。非关公署。超乎物质材料。
甚至与独身者的修行无关。也不涉及守灵。甚至超乎语言。
寺在彼岸为一只丰腴的素手托承于彤色天底。
甚至超乎动与静，无关功利。
我以全部身心这样凝视并感受着一种原始本义。
这一境界我勉为称作 —— "典"。

1994.1.25

THE NIGHT ON GRAIN BUDS

We stoop to put our noses close to a bush of wild roses.

A faint fragrance mixed with a hazy moonlight.

Now at midnight, no butterflies are joyfully competing for beauty.

While depression is still fatal to us.

Only my depression is fatal.

I must go through a hysterical nerve war and always stick to myself.

I have no fellow traveler: Who goes with me into the gem moon?

Countless farewell forms countless sections of psychological imbalance,

Now, in addition to another layer of severity.

Gray mentality makes gray life.

Gold sows hatred denaturing the pureblood Chinese.

Such a farewell day also makes flowers chill.

A depressed heart turns to the countryside may because the soul longs for
self-protection

May 22, 1994

小满夜夕

我们弯身将鼻息凑向一丛野蔷薇。
淡淡的清香混合着一袭朦胧月光。
此刻子夜，没有蝴蝶争欢。
然而苦闷横亘在我们之间仍是致命的。
唯独我的苦闷才是致命的。
每当坚守自己都得经受一场歇斯底里的神经战。
没有同路人：谁与我一同进入月亮宝石？
无数个诀别组成无数心理失衡的断面，
于今又多了一层严峻。
灰色的心态造就灰色人生。
黄金播下嫉恨使龙种变性。

如此诀别的日子花朵也让人心寒。
苦闷的心皈依田园概因灵魂渴望自卫。

1994. 5.22

THE DOMINO GAME OF MATCHSTICKS

Once upon a time, I walked back alone with a heavy heart after seeing off a friend. Near midnight, the small restaurants on the street were preparing to close for the night. Only a few adjacent small stores selling tobacco and wine remained to guard the empty night. Out of the pain and helplessness of love, I strengthened my spirit with my hands behind my back. I walked slowly toward the depths of the night listlessly (perhaps bitterly). At that time, a big man pushing a bicycle flashed out from behind the base of the overhead lamp post on the bridge fence and approached me.

"Do you have any matches? " He seemed to have waited for a long time.

I was neither frightened nor willing to answer, but I gave him a strong swing for no more disturbance. I went on slowly towards the depth of the night with my hands behind my back.

"Well, you don't have a match." When I passed by him, I heard a vicious mutter. A blow hit my whole thought, showing a glimmer of light: Match? I didn't have?...

火柴的多米诺骨牌游戏

一次，送罢友人独自心情沉重地往回走。时近子夜，街边小餐馆在清扫厅堂准备打烊，只有相邻几家出售烟酒的小店尚守着空夜苦苦煎熬。出于爱的痛苦与无奈，我背手强打精神恹恹地（也许还是恨恨地）向着夜的深处步履艰涩地踏去。那时，一个推着自行车的大汉从桥栏高架灯柱底座背后闪身而出，朝我逼近。

"有火柴吗？"他似已等候良久。

我既不感惊怖，也无心答语，只腾出手来朝他强劲地摆了摆，示意别再干扰。仍旧背手向着夜的深处步履艰涩地踏去。

"噢，你没有火柴。"与之擦身而过时听他恶狠狠地咕哝了一句。

我囫囵的思绪似乎受到一击，透出一丝亮隙：火柴？我没有？……

In an afternoon, ten days later, I was sending an express mail to the downtown postal building. I bought stamps and stick-on letters with the glue standing in an unattended counter section. At this time, a young woman dressed in style walked directly to me. I thought she was borrowing the glue. But she asked: "Do you have any matches?" Staring at her beautiful face, a woman, I couldn't see through the necessity. No, I don't. I sent a sure message. But she uncompromisingly (or even very elegantly) raised her index finger and whispered: "Shh! Just one. One match."

She turned around and walked away disappointedly and could not be seen in a hurry. I was trapped in a loss: No, I don't. We don't.

When I meet my friend again, whom I am deeply distressed about, he finally asks me: "Does it have any?" Yes, it's a match and only a match. We are being led into some holistic spiritual madness... Pain often happens.

June 16, 1994

已然是旬日之后的中午，我在市中心邮政大楼投寄一份快件。购好邮票，倚着无人值守的一段柜台用自备胶水粘贴函件。此时，一个打扮入时的青年女子确然朝我走来。我当作是与我商借胶水了。她却问道："火柴有吗？"望着她美丽的面孔，一个女子，我看不透这种必要。没有。我确然发出信息。但她决不妥协地（或竟是十分优雅地）竖起食指轻声示意："嘘！只要一根。一根。"她转身失望地走了，眨眼间消失在匆匆人流。我陷入一种不知所措的彷徨：是的，没有，我们都没有。

我曾为之深感痛苦的友人当再次晤面，也终于如此问到我了："告诉我：它有吗？"是的，是火柴，而且只是火柴。我们正被导入一种整体性的精神迷狂……痛苦是经常的事。

1994.6.16

THE MEANING OF MAZE

The theme of escape is deeply rooted.

The bud of escape penetrates into veins.

Looking for clarity, we agree to meet each other and escape from the city towards the small round hill in our memory. We set off.

At each fork, we ask: Is there a way to the small round hill?

The answer is unanimous: The way is long ahead of you. How can there be no way? All roads are way. A sincere heart can work wonders.

We are not suffering enough. Not desperate enough. It is far from the death of emotion. In other words, we are still very lucky. Thus, our escape is actually like a game.

Thus, we often fall into an interesting maze.

An elder points to the only mountain road and claims it is the small round hill.

It is not until we get up to the gap on top of the mountain sweatily and face the large and small orderly arranged graves all over the mountain when we wake up and feel so pure.

Above us, under the autumn sky, a civil aviation airliner propelled by a propeller turbine steadily flies over our heads from the vast mountains and disappears quickly. Then we watch the setting sun in the west slowly fall in our opposite direction. The orderly arranged stone tablets in the cemetery reflect the residual light as white as bones, which means serenity, blitheness and intrepidity.

October 13, 1994

迷津的意味

遁逃的主题根深蒂固。

遁逃的萌动渗透到血液。

寻找一种澄澈，我俩相邀遁逃这座城池向着记忆中的小圆山。我俩出发。

在每一条岔路，我俩打问：有通向小圆山的路吗？

回答也是众口一辞：路，在你前面早就有了。怎能没有路呢？横竖都是路。心诚则灵。

我俩还不够痛苦。还不够绝望。还远未达到情绪死亡之境。换言之，我俩尚属于十足的幸运者。因之，我俩的遁逃其实近于一种游戏。因之，我俩常常落入有趣的迷津。

直到一位长者指着唯一的一条山路，声称那里就是小圆山。

直到我俩一身汗津登上山顶豁口，面对遍山井然排列的大小坟包才如梦初醒，无比澄澈。

此时，比我俩更高，在秋空之下，一架由螺旋桨涡轮推进的民航客机正从苍茫群山那边沉稳地飞越我俩顶空，片刻悄无声息。然后我俩望着西斜的日头向着相反的方向缓慢地坠去。墓地济济一堂排列有序的碑石，反射着煞白如同白骨的余光，这意味着安详、无虑、无畏。

1994.10.13

THE BOY KISSING WITH PYTHON

It is a little boy with a python tied around his neck. At that time, he walks out of the curtain at the side of the circus for the rest of the actors and paces with measured steps like a privileged man embracing the god of a mountain in his arms. He walked from the idle crowd directly to the street and stood still, giving the plateau a sort of southern street view in summer.

It is a little boy with a python tied around his neck.

He touches the head and neck of the python with his hands alternately, and the fleck scale seems to phonate a magnificent metallic trill under his hands. The python opens its eyes wide, sticking its tongue out frequently like a lighting flash towards the boy, as if it is begging, asking, and near flattering.

He feels the call. The boy sucked up his lips and kissed them endlessly. He opens his round lips slightly to let its head gradually enter his body. People see it as a profound and earth-shaking integration experience of soul and flesh. For a moment, the boy's radiant dark eyes in love become detached and self-sufficient and turned away with a supercilious look.

Oh, the beautiful statue of a young saxophone player.

At that time, I regard the little boy kissing the python as a young saxophone player on the street. In that way, I feel the round sky has the sound of a saxophone subwoofer out of this breath, full of life and vitality. It is the harmony of humans and god, the integration of things and body, and the resonance of heaven and earth, spreading with the beautiful impression of thinking.

October 14, 1994

与蟒蛇对吻的小男孩

是一脖颈盘缠着大蟒的小男孩。那时，他从马戏班场地一侧供演
员休息的幕帷走出，就这样踱着方步如同天之骄子拥着怀中的山
林之神，从围观的闲众身边走过，径直来到街边，立定，让高原
夏日有了几分蛮方的街景。
是一脖颈盘缠着大蟒的小男孩。
他双手交替地摩挲着大蟒悠缓滑动的头颈，鳞斑在其手感之下恍
若发出华贵的金属的颤音。那蟒蛇圆睁双眼，口中，不时抽动的
信子电闪一般频频朝向孩子，仿佛是一种讨好乞怜，一种问询，
一种近似阿谀的试探。
感觉到了那种呼唤。那孩子噏起嘴唇与之对吻作无限之亲昵。他
微微启开圆唇让对方头颈逐渐进入自己身体。人们看到是一种深
刻而惊世骇俗的灵与肉的体验方式。片刻，那男孩因爱恋而光彩
夺人的黑眸有了一种超然自足，并以睥睨一切俗物的姿容背转身
去。
啊，少年萨克斯管演奏家的优美造像。
那时，我视这位与蟒蛇对吻的小男孩是立于街头的少年萨克斯管
演奏家了。从这种方式，我感到圆转的天空因这种呼吸而有了萨
克斯管超低音的奏鸣，充溢着生命活力，是人神之谐和、物我之
化一、天地之共振，带着思维的美丽印痕扩散开去。

1994.10.14

ONE HUNDRED YEARS OF ANXIETY

The morning here is always obscure, just like dusk.

Because of the "anxiety" "about being solved sooner or later" in mind, I decided to take the wheelbarrow of our neighbor, old D, to the city for delivery. Old D has removed the door plank from the hinge and loaded it on the wheelbarrow. This was the idea of the smart man who carried the door plank on a long journey to prevent thieves from entering the room. He urged me to get on the road quickly, but at this time, I could not completely remember why I had the anxiety and why I went to deliver in the town. I asked old D to wait for a moment so that I could bring back my memory. Patting my forehead, I make up a poem:

A thought flips in my heart:
Endless layers of matryoshka. Endless chains of interlock.
Oblivion is in oblivion. Remembrance is in remembrance.
Never know where to go, a thought flashes by fast.

Monologues become rocks in the mountain.
Birds look at coagulated proteins.

百年焦虑

此间的早晨总是迷蒙的，与黄昏相差无几。

因记着"迟早总得解决"的"焦虑"，决心搭乘邻里老 D 的手推车进城交割。老 D 已从户枢卸下门板往车上装载，这是那个担着门板远行以防窃贼入室的聪明人想出的主意。他催我快点上路，而这时，我却不能完全记起焦虑究竟为何了，又何以去城里交割。我请老 D 稍待，好让我钩沉记忆。我拍拍自己的脑门，居然诌出了一首诗：

有思怦然于心：
套不尽的无穷套。扣不尽的连环扣。
遗忘在遗忘里。追忆在追忆中。
永不知所往，有念一闪于忽忽。

独诰变作山中石头。
飞鸟展望在凝固的蛋白。

A grey sheep is watching all this on the roadside. When I notice its existence, it turns into a dog browsing fine grass. It becomes a harmless ram again when I won't notice its existence. Old D is urging me to go again. I tell him: An uncertain will, is like an operation with an unknown goal; what good would it do to go to the town. And you carry your door plank on the journey; even though the way is far away, you still worry about your door. But I, a homeless man, just waste my anxiety pointless, taking it as a spiritual ration. How am I not smart, and how am I not stupid...

Old D looks at me with no idea what to say.

July 6, 1995

一只灰羊在路侧瞅着这一切。当我注意到它的存在，它就变作一只啮食细草的狗。而当我不要注意它的存在时，复成为一只对我无害的公羊。老 D 又在催我上路。我对他说：不能确定的意愿，如同目标未明的操作，虽进城又何益。而你背负着自家的门板上路，路虽远，你仍在自家门前操心着呢。而我，是一个无家可归者，只是无谓地挥霍着自己的焦虑，当作精神的口粮。我又如何不聪明，我又如何不犯傻呢。……

老 D 望着我，终不知所云。

1995.7.6

THE NAUGHTY KID PLAYING IN THE WATER

I tell those who love me: You have seen the dam standing in the river ahead. You have seen that the reservoir overflows over the dam abutment and hangs a silver circular water curtain. You have heard the rumbling water hammer of the deep valley and the rumbling thunder — dark clouds are rolling from the horizon, and cold air is approaching. Great. Such a thick atmosphere. Such a unique stage. Such an opportunity can be met but not sought. I want to throw off my shoes and wade into the water to stand on the dam abutment, bowing down to the torrent to clean the dust and blood on the journey coat for you and me. I want to salvage the gold ring for you three times deliberately threw down the dam — if you test my loyalty with it. I want to release the ode to the thunder and lightning smoldering in my heart.

So, I ran to the dam abutment waterfall half-naked and stood in the middle of the dam. Suddenly, I am hijacked by a certain feeling: I have entered a situation of isolation from both river banks. I could only hear the rumbling sound of the water sky wrapped thick in the rumbling. The shadow on the land reflects a special illusion. Far away by the riverside, the one who loves me waves her cool hat and shouts at me, but I could only feel the exaggerated mouth shape but could hear nothing clearly. I become a "man in the casing" caused by an invisible giant due to my behavior.

戏水顽童

我对爱我的人说：你已看到矗立在前方河道的水坝。你已看到库容潮涨漫溢过坝肩挂起一面银白色的环形水幕。你已听到那深谷隆隆的水击，同时还有那隆隆的雷殛——乌云滚滚正从天边铺盖而来，冷气逼人。好极了。这样浓浓的氛围。这样独一无二的舞台。这样可遇而不可求的机遇。我要抛掉鞋履涉水站立在那面坝肩，躬身洪流为你我洗净征衣尘垢和血污。我要三次为你打捞出你有意抛沉水坝的金指环——如果你以此考验我的忠诚。我要释放出郁积在我心中的雷电的颂歌。

于是，我只身疾奔过去，半赤裸着踏着坝肩水瀑，在坝的中央站定。突然，我被一种特定的感觉劫持：我已进入与两岸隔绝的境况。我只听到水天隆隆的音响，并被这层隆隆厚厚包裹。陆地上的影子别有一种虚幻。远在河之干，那爱我的人挥动凉帽朝我大声吆喝，但我只感觉到那夸张的口形，什么也无从听清。我以自己的行为成了一个被无形的巨无霸所罩定的"罩中人"。

The wind is roaring. The water has turned from muddy yellow to deep dark, with frothed. The dark clouds outflank the water's surface, and there is a dangerous vastness. Flying in darkness and horror. Vertigo. I feel the waterfalls overflowing my legs continue rising at a perceptible speed; there is no way to stop. The temperature of the water has been freezing to the bone. The one who loves me stands by the riverside and opens her exaggerated mouth towards me. But at that time, my ambition to fight against fate, my great wish to release from depression, my love confession, my stubbornness like Don Quixote while facing the spiritual encirclement... and so on, all that remains is the feeling of a naughty boy playing in the water. I seem to feel my mother standing by the riverside waiting, anxiously to call me home. I feel my eyes are hot and about to shed tears, but I am very happy and bow down to quickly wash away the dust and blood on the journey coat. I hear my heart whispering: Death? What does it matter about death? I'm just a child playing in the water.

August 28, 1995

风在吼。水面已由浑黄转作深黑，翻着泡沫。乌云紧贴着水面包
抄过来，有一种凶险中的浩淼。一种森严可怖中的飞动。一种眩晕。
我感觉漫过腿肚的水瀑正以可被觉察的速度继续向上潮涨，而不
可阻遏。水温已经冷得刺骨了。爱我的人站在河之干朝我启动着
夸张的口形。但那时，我本欲与宿命一决雌雄的壮志、一释郁积
的大愿、爱情表白、直面精神围剿的那种堂·吉诃德的顽劣傻劲
儿……等等，瞬刻间只剩下了顽童戏水的感觉。我似乎觉得河之
干立候的母亲正忧心忡忡地召唤我回家。我感到两眼发热就要滴
下泪水，但我却开心之极，躬身迅疾地洗涤净征衣尘垢与血污。
我听见自己的心在窃窃私语：死亡？死亡又算得了什么？我只是
一个戏水的孩子。

1995.8.28

THE DEPRESSED REHEARSAL OF LIFE

I believe my wife is the daughter of an elder master in the ancient Arabian kingdom for unverifiable reasons. She is sitting on the ground of a brick bed. My wife leans forward. Sitting opposite her is my father-in-law, elder Arabian master. Humbly, my wife has been explaining something to him. I lie beside my wife and think I am an invisible spiritual entity. The difference between my age and my wife is something the elder master always worries about: He looks sideways and frowns occasionally. Is the disordered flowering season the sin of flowers? I hoped to end the dialogue as soon as possible, so I reached out my hand and squeezed my wife's gastrocnemius from under the quilt. I believe she has understood the silent whisper. But she is still nagging; she is very tired. Whenever this happens, her eyebrows are lovingly wrinkled, and her full forehead will flash a shadow of hesitation. But this time, I see the signs of her sudden aging at a certain time in the future. This reminds me that I will double my love when that moment comes. So my wife will recover to her original state. Listen to her gently talk to me: "Let us not disturb your peaceful cultivation anymore. We will set off for home immediately after the 'Weeping Friday' is over." I don't quite understand about the "Friday" she calls; I can only recognize that it is a necessary obligation or a complete success. I am afraid excessive sentimentality will crush her originally weak constitution. However, in any case, I should be encouraged by the coming "go home".

悒郁的生命排练

我以无从稽考的理由，相信爱人是天方古国一位长老的女儿。是
在一间炕屋席地而坐。爱人身子前倾。与之相对，即我的岳父天
方长老。恢恢地，爱人总在对他解说着某一件事。我侧卧在爱人
身边，自以为是一个不为人察知的精神实体。我清楚我与爱人年
龄的差异是长老久怀的心病：他不时地侧目，眉结双皱。错乱的
花季，岂又是花草的罪过？我希望尽快结束这场对白，故暗自伸
过手去，从被衾底下将爱人的腓肠肌捏了一把。相信她已理解这
一无言私语。但仍在唠叨着，她甚是疲倦。每当此际，眉头就可
爱地皱起，前额饱满的天庭会闪过一抹犹疑的暗影。而这一次，
我从中窥见了她在未来某一时刻倏忽衰老的迹象。这是向我提示：
当那一刻到来，我会加倍付出我的疼爱。爱人仍回复原先的状态。
听她这样款款交代："我们不要再多打扰您老的清修，一俟过了'啼
哭的礼拜五'我们就立刻启程回去。"我并不十分明白她所称之
的"礼拜五"，我仅能意识到那是一种必行的义务或功德圆满。
我担心过度的感伤会压垮她原本单薄的体质。然而，无论如何我
应该为即将的"回家"而倍感鼓舞。

When awake, I lie on a bench in a large hall room of a craftsman's workshop. But my wife went out early. Travelers come and go. But what worries me most is the shoes taken off overnight with their whereabouts unknown; I have to set off barefoot. Idle people are watching me silently with the expression of enjoying comedy. I am sure the shoe thief is hidden in the dark of the workshop; probably, the cobbler is an accomplice. But I accept this all around. Every life tries possible living choices for its own existence. The underworld is a cruel one for life.

I just stepped on a pair of cotton socks and embarked on the journey; the earth is cold and refreshing. I feel the freezing outside. The socks are thickening. Actually, my two feet are pedaling a pair of ice blocks. I no longer think about buying shoes but concentrate on going to meet my wife and "go home" early.

I climb a high mountain made of stripped stones with other people. It is a green mountain similar to the pyramids. All around the mountain are mountains in pyramidal type. What a difficult and mysterious symbol indication. The closer I get to the top of the mountain, the more I feel that I will be overturned by the mountain.

I don't know whether "Weeping Friday" is over.

But I know my wife is waiting on the other side of the mountain.

If I want to vomit because of dizziness, my memory switch is disconnected.

So I find myself waking up again "really".

Walking out calmly from the drama of drama ... of drama again

I am still a winner, after all.

当我发现自己醒来的时候，是躺在一大间设有匠人作坊的穿堂屋里的长凳。伴我的爱人提前外出了。行旅往来其间。而我不胜忧虑的是过夜脱下的皮鞋去向不明，将被迫赤脚上路。闲人正以观赏喜剧的表情默看我何以下场。我已认定偷儿就聚合在作坊暗处，估计那个皮匠定是同谋。但我认可了这种存在。每一生命都为着自己的存在而尝试可能的生存选择。黑道是生命的残酷选择。

我仅踩着一双棉袜上路了，大地冰凉沁人。感觉袜子外面的冷冻正在加厚。其实两脚是蹬着一双冰砣行进。我不再考虑买鞋的事，而专心赶路以期与爱人会合早早"回家"。

我与众人攀登在一座以条形石料砌筑的高山。是碧绿的与金字塔相类的高山。四外都是如此的类金字塔式山体。何等艰难、玄秘的符号喻示。我愈接近山巅，愈是有着一种将与高山一同倾覆的预感。

不知道"啼哭的星期五"是否过去。

但我知道爱人就等候在山的那边。

我因眩晕而觉呕吐，记忆开关随之断路。

于是我发现自己又一次"真实地"醒来。

又从戏剧的戏剧……的戏剧从容走出。

我仍不失为一个胜利者。

Nietzsche said: "Dream... If it is completed once, it will be the symbolic connection between scenery and illusion, replacing the language of the narrative poem... In our dream, we have consumed too much artistic talent." But at the moment when I stoop to put on my shoes (the stolen shoes) after getting up, I suddenly remember the creation of consumed poems that I have forgotten, and record them on the paper: It can be regarded as a person's real body of several former generations — a suspending life rehearsal. Is "suspending" anything frightening from now on?

December 4, 1995

尼采说："梦……倘若有一次延续而完成，那就将是景色和幻象
的象征联结，代替那叙事诗的语言。……梦中，我们消耗了太多
的艺术才能。"但我却在起床后弯身穿鞋（被失窃的鞋）的瞬刻，
忽又记起忘失殆尽了的被消耗的诗的创造，并记录在案：不妨看
作是一个人的几世真身——中止的生命排练。从此"中止"又何
畏之有？

1995.12.4

THE EMPTY STREET ON A COLD MORNING IN WIND

On a cold winter morning, I stand on the sidewalk near the bus stop at the intersection, waiting for a friend with an appointment. There are no pedestrians on an empty street. At the police stand in the center of the crossroad, the traffic police stand in the cold rustling wind; it takes a long time to see two or three cars stop by the roadside and wait for him to blow a whistle to pass. I just stand by the street as a temporary spectator.

Suddenly, I hear a singer's bold and sturdy baritone rising steeply from the other side of Dongheng Street; it is a local fast-paced rural ditty. The man is obviously riding in some kind of vehicle toward this side. Therefore, I feel the singing is a forced invasion, an envelopment, a loud takeoff, bearing down with the weight of Mount Taishan. I am enthusiastic and look forward to the singer's appearance once revealed. At this moment, a bus just arrived — I need to identify the friend I am waiting for from the passengers off the bus. Because of this improper behavior (I needn't have been distracted), the singer passed me like a "swift wind" carrying such a loud, explosive, soul-stirring song, gone in a flash. When I realize this omission, I turn around in a hurry to follow the tone but only see the back of the cyclist drifting away towards North Street crazily. It's the back of tall women, really beyond my

冷风中的街晨空荡荡

寒冬的清晨，我站在街头靠近十字路口公共汽车站路牌一侧的便道，恭候约好的一位朋友。空荡荡的大街了无行人。街心岗亭，交通警察立在瑟瑟的冷风里，好半天才有三两部汽车停靠路口，等候他吹一声哨子放行。我就这样立在大街边暂充一名看客。忽然，我听到歌人一声鲁莽壮实的男中音从东横街那边陡地升起，是一种当地的快节奏乡村小调。那人显然是搭乘在某种交通工具朝着这边疾驶，因之，我感到那歌唱简直是一种强行入侵，一种笼罩，一种响亮的腾飞，泰山压顶而来。我受到感奋，期待着一旦被揭晓的歌人的出现。此时，恰好一辆公共汽车到站——我需要从下车的乘客辨识出我所恭候的友人。正是这一举措未当（我本不必急于分心），那唱歌的人已像一阵"急急风"挟着如此高亢、具有爆发力、勾人魂魄的歌声，就从我耳边擦身而过，一溜烟远去了。当我意识到这一疏失，急忙循声调转头去，也只见到那踏车的歌人疯狂一般向北街飘摇远去的背影——是一块头高大的女人背影，这实在出乎我意料。她单手操把两足一阵阵快速蹬踏，

unexpectation. She holds the handlebar with one hand and pedals her feet quickly while raising her left arm high, standing up to beat heavily for her singing. The wind lifts one corner of her black headscarf highly behind her shoulder, like a black flame flapping loudly. She wears women's clothes, red cloth with white flowers, but her sonorous singing voice belongs to the baritone, which puzzles me. I regret losing my mind and not seeing her in front, so I can never solve this mystery. All this happens in a moment. She sang the fast-paced rural ditty and went away. She is like walking in a deserted field -- her field is like a dream. So when those passengers just off the bus turn a blind eye and a deaf ear to it, it can be explained as: It is just a dream, a strange flash of thought. Who would be serious about that strange flash of thought! Then the past is past, really unreal. Because the reality is not real. But I feel sadness at that moment. She sings a funny rural ditty with a strong chest resonance and a voice behind her head. But I understand she must be worried. Only in the wild running and howling, in the headscarf like black flame chasing and flapping after her, may she get a moment of relief. Therefore, her energy may also be unlimited. Oh, is that so? Then why is she sad? Why do you accept such a funny song with a sad mood?

What's more, is she a woman with a male voice or a man obsessed with women's dress?... This is so-called to enjoy life. I will never see her again, for sure. But she seems to be a happy person. Painful happiness. But in the indifferent nature of the street, this is just a flash of thought, not substantially different from any color. This may be the essence of melancholy.

January 14, 1996

而左臂高扬着，挺身为自己的歌唱重重打着节拍。她的黑色的头帕在肩后被风高高地撩起一角，如同黑色的火焰拍打有声。她穿着女服，且是红底白花女服，但她沉雄豪飞的歌声却属于男中音，这令我莫解。我极后悔一时走神没有看到她的正面形象，因此，也永远解答不了这个谜。这一切仅仅发生在一瞬间，她高唱着节奏快捷的乡野小调远去了，她像疾行在无人的旷野——她的旷野，如同一掠而过的梦幻。因此那些刚刚下车的乘客对此视而不见、听而不闻应属可以理解：那只是一个梦幻、一个怪异的闪念。谁会认真于那骤生骤灭的怪异闪念！那么过去了也就过去了，极不真实。因为现实并不真实。而我却感受到了那一刻的忧伤。她唱的是一支风趣的乡野小调，带有很浓重的胸腔共鸣、脑后音。但我明白，她肯定忧心如焚，且只有在狂奔狂噪中、在头帕如同黑色火焰随她追逐拍打中，或许才获得一刻解脱。因此，她的精力也可能是无限的。噢，是这样的吗？那么她为何忧伤？又为何以忧伤的心境接受这样一支情调诙谐风趣的歌曲？而且，她究竟是保有男嗓的女人抑或是迷狂于女人衣饰的男人？……这就是所谓的享受生活。我再不会见到她了，肯定如此。但她似乎是个快乐的人。是痛心的快乐。而在大街漠然的本性里，这也只是刹那的闪念，与任何色彩并无实质区别。这或就是忧郁的本质之所在。

1996.1.14

THE PASSER-BY

"It is a small parasitic block." He has a heavy forehead, walking on a small street built on two adjacent star-rated hotels on the outskirt of R City, amazed at the thought coming to his mind in time. In the late afternoon, the shop lights up the soft lights early in the morning. For those indulging in joy, even if it is just the mood in such light, they can feel a kind of temptation.

However, he is a passerby having no luck to do with this.

Otherwise, he is just a passerby with no luck with this.

These stores are small and unique, belonging to two industries: Flavor snacks and swimwear. The passer-by is only interested in the latter. He likes those female carcass models like stars studded in the inner wall of the shop, vivid and lifelike because of wearing various kinds of tight swimwear. However, it sometimes makes him imagine suddenly facing a wall of Peking Opera masks. He is puzzled: It is neither near an inland lake nor rivers, oceans or lakes; why is the swimwear industry so developed? He is secretly excited.

Holding his heavy forehead, he is ashamed of being just a passer-by and not staying here for long — he feels disappointment from the shining eyes of the service lady in the store, with no essential difference from the complex feelings he saw in the eyes of the "escort girl" he just met at the front door of the hotel: He could even remember the bashfulness with which the obviously fat girl put on for him in haste. He admits there must be some sensational charm. So, even if feelings are just the packaging of goods, why should we have the right to blame them for being false? Living and pleasure are equally severe.

过客

"寄生性小街区。"当时他托着沉重的额头，正走在 R 市近郊一条仰赖于两座毗邻的星级宾馆而存在的小街，为及时飘入脑海的这一念头感觉惊异。天近傍晚，商店早早亮起了温柔的灯光，对于耽于享乐的人们，即便只是这种灯光情调也能从中感受到一种诱惑的浸淫了。

然而，他属于与此无缘的过客。

或者，他也只能属于与此无缘的过客。

这些商店都娇小而别致，分属两种行业：风味小吃与泳装服饰。他仅对后者持有兴趣。他喜欢那些满天星斗似的镶嵌在店堂内壁的女人胴体模型，由于穿着各式各色的紧身泳装而格外鲜活、逼真。不过，有时也使他产生如同突然面对满墙京剧脸谱那样的错觉。他迷惑不解：这里既不濒临内湖亦不靠近江海河塘，泳装业何以会如此发达？暗暗有些激动。

托着沉重的额头，他为自己仅是羁旅此地的一名匆匆过客而抱愧——从店内服务小姐招徕的目光他感觉出了一种失望，这与他刚才在宾馆大门邂逅的"三陪女郎"眼里所见到的复杂情感似乎并无本质区别：他甚至还能记起那位身子已经明显发福的姑娘顾盼之间匆忙为他扮出的那一丝羞涩。他承认其中定有煽情的魅力。那么，感情即便只是商品的包装，我们又何尝有权责备其虚假？生存与行乐都同样严峻。

"Beauty sometimes is absolutely to appreciate suffering. "Holding his heavy forehead, he remembers the two skull bowls he saw in the tourist relics store in the hotel lobby during the day: One bowl is big, the other one is slightly smaller, in the shape of a hemisphere upside down on the glass display cabinet (the study of the former residence of French literary giant Flaubert displays half of the mummy legs), in a translucent ivory color, the vertically and horizontally connected and occluded bone seams are like river network marks emerging on the color map. The rim of the bowls is polished by the file and inlaid with silver ornaments. The price of this "artwork" is 5000 yuan. A poet at the scene tells him a human skull bowl was sold for 2000 dollars by a foreign tourist not long ago on the business street of A Temple. Now, when he thinks of these conversations again, he can't help wondering whether those skull bowls are the heads of the contemporary people hunted by "headhunters" by cunning means.

"Beauty sometimes is absolutely to appreciate evil."

He thinks like this and walks faster meanwhile. The hedonistic street he called has disappeared in the shadow of lights behind him. Beside him is a long park wall surrounded by an iron fence. This is quite a long way, without lights, as part of the suburban junction. The shade can be brewing intrigue at any time. But he has no scruples. It seems just because of the vague feeling of "ending as soon as possible", He says words with vague motives such as "good" and "well" in his mouth, neither for compliment nor curse; perhaps it is just for personal comfort because he can only be a negligible passer-by "get through" the history of human development after all, inescapable.

April 13, 1996

"美，有时径直就是欣赏苦难。"托着沉重的额头，他记起了白天在宾馆楼厅旅游文物商店看到的两只人头颅骨碗具：一只大些，一只略小，呈半球形状倒扣在玻璃展柜（法国文豪福楼拜故居书房也陈列着半条木乃伊人腿），在一种半透明的象牙色彩里，纵横连接咬合的骨缝线如同彩色地图上浮现的江河水网标记。碗口经过镂锉打磨，以银饰包镶。这件"艺术品"的价码是人民币五千元。在场的一位诗人告诉他，不久前 A 寺商业街一只人头骨碗具被一位外国旅游者以两千美金成交。现在，当他重又想起这些谈话，不由疑心起那些人头碗具材料会不会是当代"猎头者"一族以狡诈手段猎杀而得的同代人首级。

"美，有时径直就是欣赏罪恶。"

他这样思考，同时走得更快了。他称作的享乐街已经隐没在身后的灯影里。身旁是一座围以铁栅栏的公园长墙。这段路颇长，且无灯火，属于市郊衔接部。阴影里随时可能酝酿着阴谋。但他并无顾忌。似乎只是出于"尽快结束"那样模糊的感觉，他动机含混地在口里念着"好啊""好啊"这样的言语，既非赞美，亦非诅咒，或许仅是出丁对个人的安慰，因为他毕竟只能属于处在人类发展史的"渡过"中一个微不足道的过客，而无可逃避。

1996. 4. 13

THE STATE OF WORDS
(TWO KINDS OF LONELINESS: CONTENTED OR DEPRESSED)

The deepest state of consciousness, a kind of words
The eternal lights are dignified, as beautiful as a quiet girl's shining eyes.

A kind word, the alcohol diluted by life
It ignites itself in the deepest and most depressed state of consciousness,
Showing sapphire blue flowers: Auspicious, peaceful, carefree and light-
hearted.
I feel it is a half-asleep vigil,
Ethereal in the mirror and nihility.

Often, words are like the state of lamps but actually depression.
A kind of word is entered into the body by another
Similar to the double shadow of the light bulb and out of the way to peel
off or escape,
Comparable to the most shameless sexual harassment.
At that time, I was burdened with confusion -- introspection,
Feeling the loneliness of losing balance in sickness.

April 23, 1996

话语状态
（两种孤独：怡然或苦闷）

意识的最为郁闭的深境，一种话语
长明的灯火那么端庄，姝若静女含光。

一种话语，生命稀释的酒精
就在意识的最为郁闭的深境自燃，
呈示宝蓝的花朵：祥瑞、平和、无虑无思。
感觉那是半睡眠中的守夜，
缥缈在镜像与虚无。

常常，话语像灯的状态却是一种苦闷。
一种话语被另一种话语进入体内
类似灯头双影叠生而无计剥离或脱逃，
可比之于最为无耻的性骚扰。
那时我承重了迷乱——内省，
而在病态中感受失却平衡的孤独。

                                    1996.4.23

MY DEATH

Disappointed Love (I)

My friend Jia Tan tells me about this:

In an article dedicated to her, I once expressed my determination to die for my love - "Death? What the hell is death? "Facts have proved that, in theory, I have died and returned to my life. At that moment of awakening, I heard a young child singing a popular love rock song outside the window to celebrate my rebirth. He sang this love song as an adult, originally sung by a young man to his lover — "Silly sister, silly sister..." I was very moved by his singing. What kind of love experience does an ignorant child use to convey the sincerity of a silly man? That's why we, who consider ourselves mature, have more reason to endure self-torture for love without thorough understanding and transcendence?

As you know, I am doomed to walk barefoot on this long, dangerous road through the long tunnel of love, and I still have no idea of its result. And I didn't have any repentance; I still felt pain for her.

Yes, as you know, I woke up from a long sleep. I don't know when, but the sky is already bright. I don't know when the child who sings for me outside the window will leave. I was glad I had finally survived another unbearable night. I got up in a hurry to go to the toilet and wash. Then I found something unusual: Why is the dawn getting darker?

我的死亡
《伤情》之一

朋友迦檀如此对我诉说：

诚如你所知悉，我在献给她的一篇文章中曾表达过那种敢于为崇偶赴死黄泉的决心——"死亡？死亡又算得了什么？"事实证明，我至少在理论上如此死亡过了并经复苏。那时候——我是说苏醒的一刻——仿佛是为了庆贺我的再生，我听到窗外一个幼童放声唱起一首当时流行的爱情摇滚。他以模拟的成人，大胆得有点故作张扬地演唱了这首原是由一个青年男子唱给其情人的情歌——"傻妹妹，傻妹妹……"我感动极了。懵懂无知的孩童是依据何种堕入爱河的经验传达出一个傻男子的真诚？自居成熟的我们因此才更有理由死去活来地为情爱承受自我折磨而不得彻悟、超度？

诚如你所知悉，我已命定一双赤脚走在这条多磨的险途，历经爱的漫长隧道，于今仍无分晓。而我也并无一丝悔改意，仍为她而深感痛苦。

是的，诚如你所知悉，我从一个长觉睡醒，不知今夕何夕，而天已大亮。窗外为我献歌的幼童不知何时离去。我庆幸自己终于是熬过了又一不堪的长夜，匆忙起身如厕梳洗盥沐。而这时我才发现情况有点异常：这个黎明何以愈加晦暗？

Friend, I still can't forget life and death. My mind and body are too weak: ——My "daydream" completely reverses the time sequence. Rather than bear the pain soberly, I am willing to go back to sleep, even if it is a kind of sneaking, hiding, a real death. Death is also a kind of self-protection. Otherwise, how can I force the time and space of pain to be compressed into what I call a "thin slice" that has lost its thickness to achieve the disappearance of self and return to nothingness?

I thought of that innocent child when I removed my coat and prepared to sleep again. He is happy because he is still ignorant of love. But he will eventually follow the example of my predecessors. Sad? Decadent? Lack of masculinity? "Where is there grass on the horizon?"? "All women are equally gentle." However, I always stick to the only one, including her body language and breath.

Forget it. ——I comfort myself. At that time, I seemed to understand the mantra "long sleep is happiness" that the Indian Happy Bird said to the Russian warrior Sateko. So I returned to the bed almost naked, lay down, closed my eyes, and waited for my death again.

December 29, 1996

朋友，我还未能做到生死两忘。我的精神与体质也是太虚弱了：——是我的"白日梦"将时序完全颠倒。与其清醒地承受痛苦，我实在情愿重新进入到昏睡状态，即便是一种偷安、一种藏匿、一种真正的死亡。死，也是一种自我保护。不然，我以何种方式强迫将痛苦的时空压缩为我所称之的失去厚度的"薄片"，以达自我之消泯，归于虚无。

当脱去外衣准备重新入睡，我想起了那个稚气的幼童。他是幸福的，因为他还暂处于对情爱的懵懂。但他终将蹈袭前人有如我之现在。可悲吗？颓废？缺少阳刚之气？"天涯何处无芳草"？"天下女人都是同样温柔"？……然而，我总还是执着于那个唯一的她，包括她的体语、气息。

算了吧。—— 我安慰自己。在那时我仿佛对于印度幸福鸟说给俄罗斯勇士萨特阔的那句咒语"长眠就是幸福"有了一种恰中下怀的解悟。于是我近乎赤条条地重又回到床褥卧倒，紧闭双眼，等待自己再一次地死去。

1996.12.29

THE NAMELESS WORRY
Sentiment II

My friend Jatan told me this:

Yes, my friend, "The world is bustling, all for profit; the world is hustling, all for profit". Except for a few lucky sycophants or outlaws who become rich overnight, going after fame and money in the secular world, most people carrying a leather bag containing money and jewelry on the back of their necks always shy have a shallow pocket, with all savings only enough for a few meals. Some are almost crammed with so-called conscience, benevolence and the poet's pure feelings, heavy. However, they can't bear the burden and refuse to change their initial aspirations. They are free from disloyalty in their late years. Who knows, this has worried some people. I have heard some inventors of "happiness hallucinogens" ridicule them as "urban sour face and pie hole", and their behavior as such has violated the "happiness" advocated by him.

However, I only want to commend people bearing heavy burdens who are conscientious; their sighing is a warning to the order of the world.

The complicated mortal life, full of love and hate and cries and weeps, has worn away the ambition of many skin and bones from ancient to modern.

无以名之的忧怀
《伤情》之二

朋友迦檀如此对我诉说：

是的，朋友，"天下熙熙，皆为利来；天下攘攘，皆为利往"。除了极少数幸运的钻营者或亡命徒一夜暴富，在芸芸众生奔波寻食的尘埃，多数人后颈驮负着的盛装银洋铜钿的皮囊总是羞涩得很的，所蓄不过几顿饭资。其中有一部分又几乎全为所谓的良知、仁智与诗人的纯情塞满，虽是沉重得很，人不堪其负，他们却不改初志，且无晚节不忠。谁知，这倒成了某些人的心病。我曾听到某个"欢愉制幻剂"发明家嘲讽他们是"城市的苦瓜脸，是田野上的乌鸦嘴"，其行为本身就已违背了该先生奉行的"欢愉"的主张了。

然而，我独要称道那些负重而行者是世道良心，其喟然的呼叹是对人间秩序的警示。

滚滚红尘，恩恩怨怨，啼啼哭哭，消磨了古往今来多少白骨人的志气。

Yes, my friend, I am even shocked today by a model of a female body in front of a fashion shop at the crossroads, stripped of clothes and dressed nothing against the wind by the shopkeeper. The shopkeeper thought the satisfaction of the desire to peep would bring him a great fortune, so he sat soundly on the chair and chuckled. I feel sad and ashamed for all women being secretly betrayed and raped. I lowered my head and hurried past the pavement. Then I wondered if I could afford to buy freedom for my humiliated lover or warm her with my quilt and coat? But even if I can do it, more women must be abused similarly; profiteers have no mercy on them.

Yes, my friend, today is my most painful day: My lover told me she might be chosen as a bride by a wandering medicine vendor. She said not until the selection went to "the eighteenth one" she was taken fancy on by the wanderer at first sight.

Yes, my friend, mortal life is rather vulgar today. I give all the deposits of my life -- sincerity, infatuation, talent, temperament and long wait to win her heart. Still, she was flattered enough to hear the wandering medicinal vendor say, "the eighteenth one". But I am still deeply attached to her, calling her my "holy idol". She is inherently a holy idol. While money is the source of all evil.

Oh, my friend, please take all of this -- including love, the leather bag containing money and jewelry, and my unbearable pains — as a fable.

January 4, 1997, 4:00 am

是的，朋友，我今天甚至为十字街头某时装店门口一个被店主剥净衣饰、赤裸裸临风玉立的女模特儿模型而感惊恐莫名了。店主以为这种窥视欲的被满足会给他带来财源滚滚，而安坐堂前而窃窃自喜了。我为世上所有女子隐秘的被出卖、被强暴而感到悲哀与羞愧。我低下头来，匆忙走过这片铺面。当时我想，假如我有钱为我受辱的女子赎免，或以我的被衾为其裹覆？但是即便我真的能够办到，肯定还会有更多女子被以同样的方式施虐，食利者决不仁慈。

是的，朋友，今天是我最为痛苦的日子：我的恋人告诉我，她或要被一个走江湖的药材商贩选作新妇。她说，她是那个江湖客历选到"第十八个"才被一眼看中的佳人。

是的，朋友，滚滚红尘于今为烈。我以一生的蕴积——至诚、痴心、才情、气质与漫长的期待以获取她的芳心，而那个走江湖的药材商仅须说一句"第十八个"她已受宠若惊。但我仍旧深深依恋着她，称她是"圣洁的偶像"。她本也就是圣洁的偶像，而金钱才是万恶之源。

啊，朋友，请将这一切——包括爱情、包括盛放银洋铜钿的皮囊、包括我不可自拔的痛苦……看作一个寓言故事。

1997.1.4 凌晨 4 点

The SINGING OF COURTING SWAN
Sentiment III

My friend Jatan told me this:

As you know, I always go to see the mistress of this apartment — my adorable angel.

For the past few years, all the glittering spots in my emotional life, or the gloomy haze, could find some internal connection from this space. Every door, window and dust here has a sacred right to convey different messages to me. The abnormal temperature and the change of oxygen content here directly affect my heart's beating and my mind's agility. Even from knocking at the door, it is not difficult for careful neighbors to distinguish the subtle changes in my mood. This is my misfortune: Her mansion has become an existence connected with my soul and flesh, and I will not stop bleeding once we are separated.

Finally, I heard this chilling news: She will run away with someone.

Today, I hear her whistling softly, leaning against the kitchen stove: Is it because of happiness or regretful sadness?

She told me it was not an auditory hallucination, but she whistled.

寄情崇偶的天鹅之唱
《伤情》之三

朋友迦檀如此对我诉说：

诚如你所知悉，我总是去拜见这套居室的女主人——我的崇偶。
几年来，凡是我情感生活中亮丽的光点，抑或黯然沮丧的阴霾，
都可以从这一空间找到某种内在关联。这里的每一扇门窗、每一
段尘埃都有神圣权利向我传达不同信息。这里的异常气温与含氧
量的变化，都直接影响我心脏的起搏与思维的敏捷程度。甚而从
叩门的方式，细心的邻人也不难从中分辨出我情绪细微的变化。
这正是我的不幸：她的宅邸已成为与我灵肉连属的存在，一旦剥
离会流血不止。

终于，我听到这个让人颤栗的消息：她将跟人出走。

这一天，我听到她靠在厨房的灶台轻轻吹着口哨：是因为幸福还
是悲情难却？

她告诉我不是幻听，确实是她吹了口哨。

I say: This is a trade.

She says: Don't think about anything.

Oh, I'm dying of suffocation.

So, I seriously think about death — understood death: If the death of a person makes people indifferent, or is even ridiculed in words, then the act of death is equivalent to a game. But the pain of life is heavier than the game of death, so the pain has a moral significance: endure self-punishment, hate, ponder, and never be free for life. At the same time, suicide is only a one-time payment.

I know the steps of chronic death: The death of one's body is no faster than a self-destructing plant, for example, a pot of flowers, at first refuses to enjoy and accept: The fertile soil, water and warm sunshine are no longer attractive to the dying life until life escapes like a wisp of smoke.

I remember a preacher's saying: The body is only the material form of life. It is only one of the various forms of human beings.

So, should there be a purely spiritual form of life?

But I am suffering from the pursuit of spirit. My innocent body has been in pain; how can I bear the spirit of eternal life?

My material form has died, but she who I died for is still alive, — a flower will be defiled by evil.

Pain is deep into the bone marrow; it causes blood loss in the heart, sweats on the body surface, and slowly wears off my limbs and five sense organs in the dream words.

January 23 to 25, 1997

我说：这是一笔交易。

她说：你就什么也别去想。

啊，我快要因窒息而死了。

于是，我认真思考了死亡——认识死亡：一个人的死如果让人无动于衷，甚而被戏谑于言谈，死的行为已等同于游戏。但生的痛苦比死亡游戏更沉重，因此痛苦具有了道德意义，——自谴吧，含恨吧，冥思苦索吧，终生不要解脱，而轻生只是一次性到位的支付。

我知道了慢性死亡的步骤：一个人肉体的死亡并不比一株自我摧残的植物更快捷利索，譬如一盆花，先是拒绝享有、受纳：肥沃的泥土、水与和煦的阳光对于垂亡的生命不再具诱惑力，直至生命如轻烟一缕遁逸而去。

我记得一个布道者的话：肉体只是生命的物质形式。只是人的诸种形体之一。

那么，还应有生命的纯精神存在形式？

但我正因精神追求而痛苦。我无罪的肉体已为痛苦所株连，那么，永生的精神于心何忍？

我的物质形式消亡了，但我为之殉情的她还依然活着，——一朵花将为恶所玷污。

痛苦是深及骨髓的事实，让心脏失血，让体表盈汗，让我的四肢、五官在呓语中缓慢地消失。

1997.1.23—25

TWO TURTLES

If happiness is just the feeling of the environment

Pain is the real bleeding leading to heart death.

Love and not love, two climbing and falling turtles

Entangled in struggling, while the tomb of love

It is quietly consolidating and shaping up under their flippers.

This is unacceptable deformation: The mutual affinity of

The two turtles have been covered with hard armour,

They drumble, melting in the torment of each other.

I surely understand the cause of this disaster,

But it needs the courage to tell the devil's cause.

I can no longer withstand such distortion,

A row of wax tears bleaches my dejected eyes.

I heard the persuasion of friendship: Poet

You should think more about her shortcomings and even her mistakes.

And I can just recall her rare advantages as I like.

No, I also longed for the battle of free spirit out of body

Like a bare sword coexists with the everlasting fame of a warrior.

The battlefield on which today's unfortunately sacrificed warriors fight without fear,

The fight of turtles is hand to hand-between two carapaces,

Biting or licking just leaves silence behind the turtle shell.

January 29, 1997

两只龟

幸福如果只是对环境的感觉
痛苦却是导致心死的真实出血。
爱与不爱，两只攀爬跌打的龟
在折腾中纠缠未休，而爱的坟茔
正在脚蹼下悄然垒土成形。

这是不可接受的变形：两只龟
共有的灵犀已被坚甲裹覆，
行为愚钝，消融在彼此的折磨。
我当然明白这一灾变的缘由，
但说出魔鬼的诱因却需要勇气。

我再也经受不起这样的扭曲，
一行蜡泪漂白我失神的眼睛。
我听到了友情的劝喻：诗人啊
你应该多思及她的缺点以至错误。
而我尽只追忆她难得的好处。

不，我也渴望过灵魂出窍的战斗，
像赤裸的剑与勇士垂世的英名共存。
不幸今日阵亡者誓死如归的疆场，
龟的对阵却是隔着双层甲壳的肉搏，
咬啮或者舔舐只余龟板背后的沉寂。

1997.1.29

THE WOUND IS MY NOSTALGIA

Nostalgia always contains the theme of "going back home", which more or less seems sad. As if it comes to mind by chance, but for the internal needs of profound reasons. Oh, the feelings of the helpless can even make the depressed chest like a wall of iron, suddenly ringing out a loud song, — it cannot be erased from the mind; the trace of unforgettable bitterness is deeply rooted in my heart, worthy of eternal regret, while the opportunity to rectify may be lost forever. And I realized I had some experience as well.

At that time, I was lying in a bed at the bathhouse on my chest. Several elderly people had just finished bathing on other beds near me, wrapped in bath towels and crossed their knees face to face, talking about the old bathhouse and recalling the pedicure master and his daughter they knew had died for many years. Their conversation was a bit like a classroom discussion; the speech of the latter one certainly is a supplement and explanation to the former. I force myself to stop worrying for a moment, and I don't need to be angry; I just close my eyes and pretend to fall asleep, listening carefully to the ancient historical book — it is the archaic rolling wheels on the carriage of history. Distantly, I hear the bells swaying with the clop of horses in the wind. The faraway shadow has been weaved randomly with the speaker's narration in my

我的怀旧是伤口

怀旧总会包含一个关于"回家"的主题，多少有着哀婉感伤的韵味。仿佛偶然涌上心头，却为着原因深远的内在需要。啊，无奈者的感怀甚至会让郁闷的胸口像铜墙铁壁蓦然发出一声浩歌，——那不可从心头抹去，耿耿于怀的一丝酸楚如此刻骨铭心，值得永世追悔，而改正的机会却可能永远地失去了。而意识到自己也有了几分阅历。

那时，我心事重重静卧在公共浴室的一个床位，邻床浴罢的几个老者，披裹着浴巾盘膝相对，聊起了旧日的浴室，回忆起他们共同熟识的修脚师傅及其女儿都死去了许多年了。他们的谈话有点像课堂讨论，后一个人的发言，必定是对前者的补充与阐释。我强制自己暂刻刹住忧怀，也不必气恼，闭目假寐，而谛听那久远的史乘——那是历史的马车久远了的轧轹。慢慢地我听到了在风中随马蹄声摇摆的铃铎，而远逝的影子已在我的想象中随着说话

imagination. I recognize it is a high and wide bathhouse guest room, with carved beams and painted rafters, mirrors embedded in the walls around, scroll paintings hanging down, potted plants on the windowsill, and a white yak tail whisk hanging on the capital. The marble floor is spotlessly clean, the beds are arranged in order, and the bathers are first led to their beds and asked to undress, — most of their clothes are long gowns and mandarin jackets, cotton garments and cyan-collar robes, taken off and lifted up with a red paint pole by the waiter, hung high on a row of hooks on the beam. They are quietly invited to the hot water bathing pool in the back hall. The waiters are well trained, with unique skills, and their drawling, calling and answering add a bit of liveliness to the leisurely and comfortable atmosphere in the room. Scented tea and snacks are on the bedside table, and hot dishes can be fetched by the waiter from outside stalls and the hotel at any time. The bathers here always spend half a day in hot water. Therefore, going to the bathhouse is a personal enjoyment and a way to entertain guests and enhance friendship and communication. Every year when the Spring Festival approaches, the bathhouse is decorated with lanterns and streamers, welcoming guests overnight. After the bell rings for the new year, the business is meeting its real prosperity. The last group of guests is always the cashiers in charge of money from big shops. And so on.

人的叙述随意补织。听出那是一间宽大高敞的浴室客房、雕梁画栋，四周明镜嵌壁，画轴垂陈，盆栽摆设窗口，白牦牛尾拂尘挂在柱头。大理石地面一尘不染，床位整齐排列，沐浴者先被领到自己的床位，请宽衣，——也多是些长袍马褂、布衣青衿，脱下来由伙计用一根红漆撑杆挑起，高高悬挂在横梁一排衣钩，然后被请到后厅形迹不露的汤池。服务员训练有素，各怀绝技，吆喝与应答带几分拖腔拖调，为室内悠然闲适的氛围添几许闹热。床头柜几放着香茶点心，热食小炒可打发伙计去门外摊位、酒店随时端来。入浴者在这里总要泡掉半天时光。因之，请去浴室洗澡不只是个人享受，还是宴宾会客增加情谊交往的方式。每年春节临近，浴池张灯结彩，通宵接客。待年夜钟声响过，才真正到了生意红火一刻。最后一批客人必是各大商号掌管银子的账房先生。如此等等。

However, I sigh to myself: The nostalgia of the old bathing guests is just the taste of old things, greatly enjoyable; my impression has already included participation, but what have I to do with it? My nostalgia is unique and secret, with only deep wounds, indisposed to touch or to talk to others, but the feeling just emerges heavily towards me; I haven't got a moment to escape even in the bathhouse. But I hope there could be Lethe water to help me freeze and benumb. Otherwise, as a poet said: "Let the most beautiful woman on earth/conceive herself again" — I would rather be a child again so that I can make up for my regrets in previous generations. Or, I should return to the Schloss sans souci forever — where life comes from, and here, it is a more complex and profound subject about "going back home". But at present, I am just a preoccupied wanderer on my chest in the bathhouse, not aware of where the countryside and the prospect are, listening to the elderly's chattering.

February 1, 1997

然而，我却暗自叹息了：老浴客们的怀旧仅是对旧事的品味，无比滋美，我的意念已含参与，却与我何干？我的怀旧是独有的、隐秘的，只有深深的伤口，轻易不敢主动触碰，也不忍对人言，只是那怀旧之情依然要心事重重地袭来，即便是在浴室亦不容我有片刻逃避。我但切望有一种忘魂汤赐我凝冻与麻木。不然，如能像一位诗人所云："让世上最美的妇人／再怀孕自己一次"，——我实在宁肯再做一次孩子，使有机会弥补前生憾事。或者，永远回到无忧宫——人生所自由来处，而这，是一个更为复杂深邃的有关"回家"的主题。但目前，我仅是浴室中一个心事浩茫的天涯游子，尚不知乡关何处、前景几许，而听着老人们的絮叨。

1997. 2.1

IN THE SEASON OF AUTUMN,
DEAD BUTTERFLY AROUSES SIGH OF REGRET

Time is silent while the color of autumn deepens a bit. The leaves on branches have heard the call of approaching bleak autumn wind in the north, and the departure date is better not to postpone, even though it is promised to linger for a while;— "Drinking to pipa songs, the soldiers are summoned to fight". With a sigh, the spirit drifts away from the dwelling bole, and the wandering soul is already floating beyond the west of Yangguan Pass. It infects unbelievable, and then more leaves follow the course. What a shocking heroic scene: The air is filled with noise from distant travelers' bustling footsteps!

When the border women I know to walk through the door I attached myself to, the courtyard and even the corridors have already been dotted with fallen leaves. In this dotted pattern, a butterfly in ochre yellow is inlaid between, unknown to her and unknown to me, where the woman's soft embroidered shoes just step on. I hear her scream and know something dreadful has happened.

秋之季，因亡蝶而萌生慨叹

一叶知秋，而秋色更深了几许。枝头的树叶已经听到北边那逼近的萧瑟秋风的召唤，不好将行期再延搁推迟了，哪怕只是应许再缠绵片刻，——"征人欲饮马上催"，一声叹息飘离寄身的枝柄，那游魂已在阳关以西。这真如梦也似的感染，然后有更多的树叶步其后尘，其壮烈让人触目惊心：怎么，空中尽是远行者赶路的杂沓之声！

我所相识的边城妇人当其从我寄身的门隅走过，庭院以至廊庑早有落叶斑斑点点地铺陈点缀着了。在这一图案样式的斑斑点点之中，有一只赭黄色的蝴蝶镶嵌其间，不为她知，亦不为我知，妇人绵软的绣履恰好踏足其上。我听到她尖叫一声知道有了惨烈的事件发生。

A butterfly in ochre yellow. I walk to gently pick it up from the ground, taking care of it with my fingertips, an intact body still, as lively as back to life it will. This should be attributed to the softness of women's embroidered shoes. But she keeps blaming herself. I give her my comfort: "Why should you? The deceased died well and completely, and the spirit lives eternal life; this is also a happy lot. I will build a nest for its eternal dream in my poem book." However, the woman is a sincere believer and still regrets her careless mistakes. Her cautiousness challenges my impatience, and a sigh of regret suddenly arises, so I tell her:

-- You don't need to, really don't, Ms, look, the autumn wind is getting stronger and stronger, and fallen leaves are lying down around us with a last sigh. We are talking among the breath of death. Everything is in a process; what should happen is inevitable. What has happened still goes on. The butterfly is resting on the path you must pass. It must be waiting for your embroidered shoes' gift of a soft moment. Just like the poem of my poet friend, "Horses step on flower, /the flower/still kisses the hoof wildly", why not possible? She will be grateful for this... Well, even if you have no intention to say this, even the living are crying in such bleak weather, as if heaven has sent a message of recalling people. This insect

是一只赭黄色的蝴蝶。我走去从地上轻轻揭起，呵护在我指端，其体态仍完整如初，栩栩欲活。这应该归功于妇人绣履的绵软。但她只是责备自己。我为之劝导："何必呢，死者死得其所，亦死得其体，虽死犹生，这也是死者的福气。好了，我将在我的诗册为其永生的梦筑一间巢。"然而，妇人是一笃诚的教徒，仍在不尽地痛悔她不慎中的过失。她的小心让我有了几分不耐，于是一段慨叹陡然萌生，如此我对她说道：

—— 不必了，真的不必了，妇人。你瞧，秋风愈来愈烈了，落叶带着临终叹息在我们周围相继倒仆，我们是凭听着死亡气息进行谈话。一切皆属过程，凡应发生者皆不可避免。凡已发生者仍将如是。蝴蝶在你必经的小径休憩，想必正是为着恭候你绣履瞬间绵软的恩赐，好如我一位诗人朋友的诗句"马群踏倒鲜花，/ 鲜花 / 依旧抱住马蹄狂吻"，怎么不可能呢，她将为此而感恩……好了，即便你无意此说，这样凄冷的天气，连活人都在啼号，看作上苍又发出了收人的信息，这虫豸无论受你伤害与否至此应必

will surely die whether you hurt it; it has lived its best, so why should you feel guilty? And I have lost the small and delicate heart of mercy like you do. I'm a bit tired of the world. You see, the change of seasons and the move of stars every year in the human world are just the running routines of conventional patterns from ancient to modern, only adding to ages in body and face... Everything is in process. Like the stomach and intestines digest food like sexual love is acquired without learning, the stinky desire is copied by the evil nature generation after generation, and decaying life rejects people like a wide open dirty mouth; no many wonder versions of "the Flood" and "Armageddon" prophecy in different national legends happen to hold the same view... Death may be liberation or purification. My destination has already been determined, and I am not afraid. But a sign is equally true: As long as babies are born steadily, the world will never come to an end, even if sufferings are inevitable; as long as flint still remains, sparks will never burn out, -- but this law seems to have become a secret rather be felt but humiliating to be expressed...

The leaves fly away like butterflies.

Butterflies fly away like leaves as well.

This season, poets call it "melancholy autumn".

November 23, 1997

死无疑，也是尽其天年了，又何须负疚不已？而我已没有了你如此小巧细腻的肚肠。对于世间我已存几分厌倦。你瞧，那每年一度呈现于人境的寒来暑往、斗换星移只不过是古今千篇一律运作不止的套式，催人老丑而已。……一切皆属过程。像肠胃要消化美食，像性爱不学而能，发臭的欲望被猥劣的根性一代一代复制，窳败的生活就像洞开的臭嘴让人嗒然若丧，难怪世间不谋而合流传下来这许多不同民族版本的"大洪水"传说以及"末日审判"预言。……死亡倒可能是一种解脱或净化。我的终点早已确定，处之坦然。但是有一种征象却是同样真切：幼婴在，人世将无穷尽，即便仍不免于痛苦；燧石存，火种也不会死灭，—— 而这一定理现今似乎成了一个只可意会而耻于言传的秘密。……
树叶如同蝴蝶一齐飘失。
蝴蝶如同树叶也一齐飘失。
这个季节，诗人称作"悲秋"。

1997.11.23

译者简介   孙继成，山东理工大学外国语学院副教授，硕士研究生导师。主要研究领域为口述史研究、国际汉学、典籍翻译及现当代文学英译。

马晓，山东理工大学外国语学院MTI笔译专业研究生。主要从事文学翻译和典籍英译研究。

ABOUT
TRANSLATORS   **Sun Jicheng**, Associate Professor, School of Foreign Languages, Shandong University of Technology. His research interests mainly cover oral history research, English translation of Chinese classics and English translation of modern and contemporary Chinese literature.

Ma Xiao is a graduate student majoring in MTI Translation at the School of Foreign Languages, Shandong University of Technology, specializing in literary translation and English translation of Chinese classics.

审校简介　　　　　约翰·德鲁，英国诗人和研究生导师，于剑桥大学英语系获得博士学位。约翰和他的妻子冉妮（Rani John）曾在多个国家多所大学里教授诗歌写作、戏剧写作和戏剧表演。

ABOUT THE PROOFREADER　　　**John Drew**, a poet and tutor, has earned his PhD in English Department at University of Cambridge. John has taught poetry writing in different universities in the world with his wife, Rani John, teaching drama writing and performing.

图书在版编目（CIP）数据

昌耀诗歌英译选：汉英对照 / 杨四平主编. -- 上
海：上海文化出版社，2023.6
（当代汉诗英译丛书）
ISBN 978-7-5535-2745-1

Ⅰ.①昌… Ⅱ.①杨… Ⅲ.①诗集－中国－当代－汉、英 Ⅳ.
①I227

中国国家版本馆CIP数据核字(2023)第080779号

出 版 人：姜逸青
责任编辑：黄慧鸣　张　彦
装帧设计：王　伟

书　　名：昌耀诗歌英译选
作　　者：杨四平
出　　版：上海世纪出版集团　上海文化出版社
地　　址：上海市闵行区号景路159弄A座三楼　201101
发　　行：上海文艺出版社发行中心
　　　　　上海市闵行区号景路159弄A座二楼　201101　www.ewen.co
印　　刷：苏州市越洋印刷有限公司
开　　本：889×1194　1/32
印　　张：10.75
印　　次：2023年6月第一版　2023年6月第一次印刷
书　　号：ISBN 978-7-5535-2745-1/I.1055
定　　价：68.00元
告 读 者：如发现本书有质量问题请与印刷厂质量科联系　T：0512-68180628